CLEAR TO PARTLY CLOUDY

A Novel

By

J.S. Smith

CLEAR TO PARTLY CLOUDY
BY J.S. SMITH

Prologue

"Hurry up, Emily. Daddy's waiting to see us. We don't want to miss our flight," June Reynolds admonished her four-year-old daughter, Emily. She quickly ran a hair brush through her long, blonde hair and straightened her slacks (one of Josh's favorites) over her shapely legs. She checked her watch, not wanting to miss this chance to be with Josh, the love of her life. Josh had left town to attend a weeklong business conference. Now that the meeting

1

was coming to a close, June and Emily were traveling to join him for a few days of relaxation.

Before Josh had left home, he had written a poem to June, as he often did. It was a form of emotional release for him to write poetry.

> This morning I watched a bird
> soaring overhead, riding the
> thermals through the sky. Where
> was he heading? Was he going
> home to his mate?
>
> I boarded a plane and flew away
> from you, leaving my heart behind.
> How I would like to be free like
> that bird and fly on wings, back to
> my love.

After reading this poem, June carefully folded it and placed it in her purse.

"I want to take Jocko," pleaded Emily, picking up her cherished stuffed monkey.

"Okay! But the Uber driver is here and we don't want to miss our flight."

Emily began looking for Rowdy, the family's charcoal labrador retriever, and asked, "Isn't Rowdy coming with us?"

"No, he's staying at the kennel where we took him yesterday. He'll be fine. Now, come on, no more questions, we have got to go." June, becoming more anxious, realized that she had raised her voice when answering Emily.

June gathered up Emily, taking a look around for any missed items to pack. Satisfied, she placed the bags by the front door where the Uber driver grabbed them and placed them in the trunk of the car.

"What time is your flight?" asked the driver.

"Three o'clock," June answered.

"You will make it just fine," he replied.

June thanked him, and then feeling more relaxed, she turned to Emily, gently taking her hand and said, "Daddy's

3

going to be waiting to pick us up when we get there." Emily was full of questions. "Can we go to the zoo? I want to go swimming!"

June's heart melted as she studied her blonde-haired, blue-eyed daughter, who was affectionally holding Jocko to her chest. "One thing for sure," June thought, "No matter wherever Emily went or whatever she did, she would always have Jocko with her."

"We'll see, Sweetie," said June. "I am sure that Daddy has lots of fun things planned for us to do."

June took a deep breath and leaned back in the seat, hoping to get a moment's rest. Before she realized it, they had arrived at the airport.

As the driver took their bags out of the cab, he smiled and said, "You sure have a cute daughter; how old is she?"

"She is four." June smiled as she responded and handed him the fair and tip.

"Come on Sweetheart, we have to check in." Emily clutched her mother with one hand and Jocko with the other.

They checked their bags and received the boarding passes. By the time they had passed through security and arrived at the gate, their flight was already boarding. One of the flight attendants helped them to their seats. Emily sat in the middle with June seated next to the window.

Emily checked out her surroundings then looked at her mother and said, "I want the window."

"You can have it when you say the magic word," replied June.

"Please," Emily said, smiling.

June smiled back and traded seats with her.

A young man who occupied the aisle seat, snickered.

The plane began to taxi. June watched Emily with both amusement and compassion. Emily had never flown before and displayed startled expressions at each bump, shudder and clank that the plane made. "It's okay," June reassured Emily. "It always makes a lot of noise when it takes off."

The plane completed its taxi and then accelerated down the runway into liftoff. June saw the look of wide-eyed amazement on Emily's face. In a few minutes, the plane

5

reached sufficient height and leveled off with only the hum of the engines as testament of its movement. The seat belt light went off and the man in the aisle seat opened up his laptop computer.

Emily played in her seat with Jocko, telling him not to be afraid; that they would soon be seeing Daddy. She also colored in the coloring book her mother had bought her just for the trip.

June drifted in and out of sleep throughout the captain's welcome and the flight attendant's instructions in the case of emergency.

She smiled as her thoughts drifted back to the time when she and Josh first met. It was in college at a mid-semester party. Looking around the room she realized that most of her friends were married, or at least engaged at this point. But at age 23 she had no desire to settle down. Gazing around the room of noise-filled gaiety, she decided to find a quiet place to sit and rest. She noticed a man leaning back in a chair and on impulse she said, "Not your cup of tea? Not mine either." As he looked up and turned, her eyes met those of a good-looking man, and suddenly all the world around her seemed to dissolve. They stared at each other, ignoring everything else around them.

In the back of her mind, she knew she would never look at anyone else quite the same as she did him. Attracted first to his good looks; the dark brown hair and light blue eyes which created a uniquely delightful contrast drew her in, but his beautiful warm smile is what made her heart sink. It seemed her prayers were answered when he began speaking to her. He introduced himself, telling her his name was Josh Reynolds; and she in turn said hers was June Marchman. A casual and easy conversation began. She learned that he was twenty-six and a graduate student. Later she found out that like her, he had been in several relationships but was still single. As they spent the rest of the evening talking with one another, it became apparent of how similar their hopes and dreams were.

June was abruptly awakened from her reverie by a loud noise and a sudden rocking of the plane.

"Mommy, what's happening?" Emily cried out.

"It's okay, honey. I'm sure it's just the weather," June responded, not wanting to add her own fears to those of her daughter's.

"Ladies and gentlemen, please make sure that your seat belts are fastened. We are experiencing some turbulence. I will let you know when it is over," the pilot announced.

Suddenly, there was a metallic ripping sound followed by violent pitching from side to side. The captain's voice came on again, this time seeming much more anxious.

"We are experiencing some technical difficulty. Please stay in your seats. We will be making an emergency landing. I will update you as soon as possible."

June noticed that one of the attendants had picked up the phone and was evidently communicating with the pilot as the expression on her face became gravely concerned. In the next moment the aircraft rolled to one side and the nose dropped as it began to lose altitude.

June grabbed Emily's hand as the plane continued to accelerate downward on its side. Some of the overhead luggage bins had come undone and their contents spilled out onto the passengers below. The cabin became a den of noise from the passengers' uncontrollable screams.

"What's happening, Mommy? I'm afraid!" Emily cried.

June looked at Emily who was clutching her toy monkey, "It's okay, Emily. I'm here and won't let anything bad happen to you. I love you so much!" Then in a moment of blinding clarity and resignation she pictured her husband's face and whispered, "I'm so sorry, sweetheart. Please don't forget how very much I love you."

Josh Reynolds heard the phone ring and hurried over to answer it, thinking it might be June.

"Hello? Mr. Reynolds?" said a man's voice.

"Yes," Josh responded.

"Mr. Reynolds, this is Sergeant Moore with the highway patrol. Sir, I'm afraid I have some bad news for you about your family. I don't know how to tell you this. There was a plane crash up in the mountains."

Josh sucked in his breath with a gasp, before the man could go further, he immediately asked, "What about my wife and daughter? Are they okay?" His voice was muted, hesitant and shaky.

Josh's face turned ashen as he heard the words that his wife had not survived. However, a warm flush went through him as he was told his daughter was alive, with only non-life-threatening injuries.

The sergeant heard a gasp of breath and asked, "Are you all right, Mr. Reynolds?" After catching his breath, Josh replied, "No, damn it, I am not all right! I've just lost my wife, my dreams, and hopes, and YOU want to know if I'm, okay?" There was silence while Josh tried to compose himself. "I'm sorry, Sergeant. I know you are just doing your job. I'm sure this is hard for you too." There was another pause. Then Josh asked in a weakened, shaky voice, "How badly is Emily hurt?"

"It is truly a miracle that your daughter survived. It seems she was still strapped in her seat when she was thrown from the plane on impact and landed in a snow bank. That's what saved her life. Except for some exposure to the cold, she seems to be okay. She may be suffering from shock since she hasn't spoken at all."

Josh and the sergeant talked about the crash for a few moments more and Josh was told where June's body was being taken as well as which hospital Emily was in. Thanking the sergeant, he hung up the phone. Staring transfixed for several moments before collapsing into a chair, Josh had the eerie sense of being a deflated balloon. He put his face between his hands as he began to sob uncontrollably.

CHAPTER 1

Josh stood on the front porch of his cabin and watched the storm clouds as they rolled his way, accented by the rumble of thunder echoing across the mountains. Ever since he was a child, he had found exhilaration in the awesome power and beauty that rain storms displayed. It was the main reason that after the death of June, he had decided to bring his daughter Emily and their dog, Rowdy, to share the love affair that he had always had with the mountains. He loved the storms that seemingly popped up out of nowhere most afternoons. He would sit in one of the two chairs in front of the fireplace, looking out the window to watch the rain fall through the pine and aspen trees, fascinated by the soft, dappled, greenish light.

When he was a child, he would entertain himself by sitting on his parents' screened porch during a rain storm and pretend he was the captain of a ship or an airline pilot, braving the elements to bring his craft and all on board safely home. Often his fantasies involved saving a beautiful damsel in distress.

His parents would shake their heads and worry about his overactive imagination. His older brother, Mark, was dramatically the opposite of him. Mark was gregarious, athletic and popular. Even as an adolescent Mark seemed to always be up to any task and never displayed fear or lacked confidence. Mark had the body of an athlete, lean and muscular, while Josh still had the body of a pre-teen. This, coupled with Mark's blonde hair and brown eyes, gave him the look of a young Adonis, a fact his mother often mentioned. Josh did not resent growing up in his brother's shadow; rather he looked up to him with a reverent adulation. His brother always treated him with respect, and Josh was grateful for that. Mark was the star quarterback in high school and had gone on to play ball in college. He was not just a jock, but a good student as well. He might have gone on to play pro ball, but in his senior year he suffered a career ending injury. He parlayed his academic success into a graduate degree in engineering and landed a job with a large firm that was involved in classified government research.

Unfortunately for all his physical and mental prowess, his social life was in shambles. Mark had been married and divorced twice. After their parents had both been killed in a car accident, they had received a sizable amount from the insurance company settlement as well as their parents' will. Josh managed very well; however, Mark came to him on several occasions asking for financial help. Josh suspected that Mark's finances were in shambles. This puzzled Josh since his brother had such a good job. However, he asked few questions and helped his brother out whenever he could. After the death of June, they had lost touch. He had not heard from his brother in nearly a year.

Josh was jarred from his thoughts as Emily entered the room. "Looks like it's going to be a big one," Josh said as she came to stand beside him. Then reaching down, he patted their labrador retriever, Rowdy, who usually stayed close by Emily's side. Emily nodded but did not reply. She had not spoken since the accident, nor would she let go of her stuffed monkey Jocko. The doctors all agreed that there was nothing physically wrong with her. They said it was a post-traumatic stress reaction to the accident and her mother's death. They assured Josh that, given time, she would outgrow it. He could only pray that they were right.

"Better batten down the hatches," he said, putting his arm around Emily as they headed back inside to close the windows. He left a window cracked open on the opposite side away from the storm so he could smell the rain-scented air. Even though his childhood had long since passed, he still loved the smell of the clean, fresh oxygen-enriched scent that rain storms produced.

The two-bedroom, one bath cabin he had bought looked like it belonged in a picture postcard advertising a mountain retreat. It seemed as if, so the real estate agent had said, that it was "carved out of native trees" that had been treated to help make them fire and weather proof. The rocks used in the fireplace, chimney, and outside trim around the base were carried from the stream that ran nearby. It had been updated with electricity, solar panels and a backup generator. Also included was the addition of running well water, a cistern and septic system. The roof was metal and could be noisy, especially when it hailed, as it often did. The cabin floor was wood planks worn smooth from years of use. It was furnished with utilitarian, everyday furniture, the kind June would have described as "attic." The truth was that Josh loved it here, especially with the solitude it offered.

After June's death, nearly a year ago, he found he could no longer face the prospect of going back to their home without her presence. He tried immersing himself in his work at the insurance company, staying late, and keeping busy with projects around the house, but to no avail. His drive was gone; and he felt guilty about not spending more time with Emily. Everyone said, "Just give it some time," but he knew there would never be enough time to recover from what he had lost. Finally, the realization that he had to get away and make a clean break from the constant reminder of his loss became clear. He sold the house along with its furnishings, and cashed in his 401K. All that, along with the large insurance settlements he had received from both his parents and June's death, made it possible for him and Emily to leave their life behind and try to start anew, thousands of miles away.

The wind arrived first, causing the trees to dance back and forth, swirling leaves and vegetation about. The debris stirred up by the wind pelted the windows and doors, randomly making a drumming sound. The dark clouds blocked out the afternoon light.

"Better turn on some lights," he instructed Emily, as Rowdy barked in agreement.

He lit the oil lamp that hung from the center beam and several candles on the table by his easy chair, preferring their soft glow to harsher artificial lights. He moved magazines from his favorite chair, an old overstuffed leather wingback. Propping his feet up on the ottoman, he settled back and turned on the radio.

Emily sat down in a chair next to him holding the stuffed monkey Jocko, her constant companion ever since the accident. The rescuers found it interesting that she had not let it go. Rowdy circled and laid down on the floor between them. As Josh reached down to pat Rowdy, he said, "I guess we have this down pretty good, don't we, old boy?"

Suddenly lightning flashed and a booming clap of thunder startled the three of them as rain began coming down in sheets across the front of the cabin. Emily's face was stricken with fear. She was extremely edgy since the crash and loss of her mother. Josh wished she had the ability to speak so that he could know exactly what she was thinking. He reached over to give Emily and Jocko each a pat on the shoulder to reassure them both that everything would be all right. Rowdy raised his head looking toward the door and then settled back down on the hooked rug beside the chair.

Josh leaned back in his chair, lost in his thoughts as he watched the raindrops roll down the window pane. He reached down to pick up the tablet beside him and began writing.

I sit by my window watching raindrops form and slide down the panes. There are two that begin their journey at the same time, rolling along, parallel on a downward path. Occasionally they detour around some detritus that sticks to the glass. Suddenly they veer towards each other, gaining speed, until they merge together in an aqueous embrace, becoming one as they move along on a straight course. I think of you and realize that my life was like that lone drop, bouncing around erratically until you came along and our lives merged into one stream of life and love.

He placed the poem in a photo album, looked up at the ceiling for a moment, then reached down and patted Rowdy's head saying, "Pal, I think you've got the right idea." Attempting to relax, he laid his head back, letting the sound of the rain lull him into deep thoughts.

CHAPTER 2

His mind returned to the night that he first met June at the university when he was a graduate student and she was a senior. He never belonged to a fraternity, but his roommate Jimmy did. There was a big mid-semester party put on by all of the fraternities and sororities. Jimmy relentlessly nagged Josh to go as his guest.

"Come on, man, it'll do you good. There's gonna' be a lot of hot babes there."

"I need to study. I have exams coming up," Josh protested.

"All work, as they say, will make Josh a dull boy," Jimmy laughed. "What you need is a little action; a little strange stuff. You can study tomorrow. Besides, you won't see Polly there. She went home yesterday."

Polly and Josh had been seeing each other since last spring, and over the summer their relationship had migrated from friendship into passion. It was a great sexual experience and he could not wait until they were together again, exploring all the delights he had only dreamed about. He realized that she had much more experience in that department than he did. When school began in the fall, he was forced to devote more of his energy to his studies; something Polly was not prepared to accept. She liked attention and had no trouble finding it. One day he called her and a male voice answered the phone. From that moment on, their relationship began to unravel. He began to understand what she was all about. Still, it hurt him when he was not around her. The realization that she would not be attending was the main impetus, along with Jimmy's nagging, that made him decide to go to the party.

The room was full of people, many of whom were dancing to loud music being played by a live band. A lot of bodies were slumped here and there on couches and floor, some obviously drunk, and others on their way. Josh looked around for Jimmy, but he had obviously already disappeared into the crowd. This definitely was not something Josh cared for and he chastised himself for having let Jimmy talk him into coming.

Off the main room was a hall lined with chairs. Josh grabbed a beer and headed that way. Sitting down, he took a swallow of his beer; then setting it down beside him and closing his eyes, he tilted his head back into the soft fabric of the chair.

"Not your cup of tea? Mine either," came a female voice.

He opened one eye, and then gulped as he looked into the eyes of a very lovely young woman whose face was highlighted by long, blonde hair. He could not help comparing her to Polly. This girl had a classic kind of beauty, while in retrospect, Polly looked common and hard.

The girl glanced down at Josh, saying, "I don't understand what enjoyment they get out of music so loud that no one can hear a thing, and drinking so much that they can't remember what they did until the next morning."

"I agree," he nodded, as he sat up in his chair.

Pointing to the chair next to him, she asked, "Mind if I sit down?"

"Hey, it's a free country," he said immediately feeling stupid for having given such a flippant and trite response.

Holding out her hand, she said, "By the way, I'm June Marchman."

"Josh Reynolds," he responded, shaking her hand. For a fleeting moment, the thought crossed his mind to not let go of that hand.

"So, tell me, Josh Reynolds, if you don't enjoy this kind of thing, why did you come?"

"A friend talked me into it," Josh answered with a shrug of his shoulders.

"Same here. Besides, my sorority requires attendance."

"Oh, you're in a sorority?"

"Yes, I am, but don't judge me by that. I did it mainly to please my parents. They think it will have a long reaching effect on my future; how about you?"

"I'm not a Greek. Like I said, I only came because my friend insisted."

June, pointing her finger toward the frenzy in the next room replied, "Well. I'm glad you came. Otherwise, I would not have had an excuse to sit here with you. I would have had to endure that madhouse in there."

Josh was about to respond when a couple of giggling girls appeared.

"There you are. We wondered where you disappeared to," they said, glancing at Josh, then dismissing him and looking back at June. They grabbed her hand, pulling her up.

"Come on! We have someone who wants to meet you."

As she was being led away, June turned back to look at him. Smiling, she said, "It was nice meeting you, Josh. Thanks for letting me sit with you."

"Any time," he answered, meaning it.

He did not see her again for several weeks, but he thought of her often. He was walking across campus when he heard someone calling his name.

"Hi, Josh, remember me?" came a familiar voice.

He turned around and saw June walking towards him. "Hi, June," he replied, trying to look and sound casual. In truth, he was anything but that.

24

"Where are you going?" she asked.

"I just got out of class. I thought I might get some coffee."

"That sounds like a great idea. Mind if I join you?"

"No!" Then, trying not to appear overly eager he said casually, "Not at all. That would be nice."

Over the next several weeks, Josh would frequently run into June on campus. She was usually with a group of girls, but would excuse herself in order to come over to chat with him. They became friends, spending more and more time talking about classes, professors, the world's situation, or just enjoying each other's company. Gradually, Josh realized that his feelings were becoming more than just friendship. He finally summoned up the courage to ask her out. "Do you think... I mean, do you think, possibly you might consider doing something with me next Saturday night? You know, a   date," his voice trailed off.

"You mean a real date?"

"Oh, yes, I mean...," he said, feeling flushed.

"I would love to. I was wondering if I was going to have to ask you," she revealed, with a laugh.

He was in heaven! This girl was unlike any other he had ever met. She was bright, funny, and best of all, she seemed to genuinely like him. Their dating started out casually; just two good friends sharing common interests and enjoying each other's company. Gradually their relationship began to change. They found that even when they ran out of things to talk about, they still felt comfortable together. He realized that this was what real love was: a desire to be with each other, no matter what the situation. Just knowing that you are happy with the one person who means more to you than anything else in the world is what real happiness is about. He felt that if they were locked in a room alone and he was forced to spend eternity there with her, it would be enough. One Sunday afternoon they were sitting on the couch in his apartment, drinking cheap wine and listening to music. Suddenly, she leaned over and kissed him. They had kissed before, but without passion. It had always been as friends, not lovers. He was caught by surprise, but he

26

returned her kiss with increasing ardor. Soon they were caught up in the heat of passion and there was no stopping, as it progressed to its inevitable conclusion. He knew from that time on their relationship had taken a different direction. Friendship had erupted into passion, and from that gradually grew a profound new kind of relationship; one based on love, respect and mutual admiration.

They spent the rest of the semester in a kind of halcyon bliss, and when he went home for the Christmas break, he wasn't sure he could endure the separation. They called and wrote each other, and made plans for the spring semester at school. When they returned, it was even more consuming. They no longer talked about me or you, but about us. Josh sent her one of the poems he loved to write as a form of emotional release.

> Has the earth stopped spinning?
> Are the clock hands frozen?
> Has the universe ground to a halt?
> Time has slowed to a standstill,
> only my heart beats faster

as I wait in anxious longing,

til we are together and I can

once again hold you in my arms.

When spring break arrived, they could not bear the thought of being separated and opted to spend the time together, rather than go home.

June lay with her head resting on Josh's shoulder. They had just finished making love when suddenly she said, "I don't want to go home. I can't stand the thought of being away from you all summer."

"Me either," he replied, hugging her. He was quiet for a moment, then rolled over towards her and said, "Marry me."

Stunned, she looked at him and asked, "What did you say?"

"Marry me. I know it's sudden, but it's something I've wanted to ask you and I can't think of any better time. We both will be graduating at the end of this summer and I don't want to start out into the world without you."

"Yes, my darling! Oh yes, of course I'll marry you!" Laughing, she said, "I wasn't sure I heard you right. I want to spend this summer and all of the summers to come with you!" June rushed into his arms, embracing him as they kissed passionately. They stood together, swaying, both lost in the euphoria of the moment.

The wedding took place in June, right after school was over. They both enrolled in summer classes in order to finish as soon as possible. The wedding was held in the chapel on campus with their families and a few friends attending. Josh's brother Mark, who had just received a divorce from his wife, created some problems with his inebriated condition, but overall, everything was perfect. Immediately after the wedding was over, June moved into his apartment. They both found jobs, staying busy between classes. Both of them were tired and haggard, but their incredible love for each other made it all worthwhile.

Josh was suddenly shaken from his reverie by a loud clap of thunder. He was surprised to discover that he had been crying. The room seemed to have become cold. He stood up and walked to the fireplace where he stopped momentarily to study the pictures of the wedding and the one of June and Emily that were on the mantel. Next to it was the carved box that held June's ashes. Enduring as much of the incredible pain as he could bare, he breathed a sigh, and reached down to pick up a log. He hoped Emily did not see him wiping the tears from his eyes.

"It's a little chilly. Guess I'd better put another log or two on the fire," he said as he walked over to the fireplace. Reaching up and patting the box with June's ashes, he said to himself, "I love you darling, and I miss you." He took a deep breath, then turned and asked Emily, "Are you hungry? I could eat a porcupine!"

She smiled, nodded her head in affirmation and Rowdy answered with a bark.

Laughing at Rowdy, Josh said, "You are always hungry!"

He went into the kitchen and poured some dog food into Rowdy's bowl, then proceeded to open a can of beef stew for himself and Emily. When they sat down to eat, he turned on the radio. He rarely paid attention to it, finding little interest in the outside world. This place was all he cared about, but he found some comfort in the sound it produced. Sometimes it helped expel his loneliness. He did listen when the weather came on and there was talk of the first major spring storm predicted to arrive in a few days.

CHAPTER 3

Amanda Pace was in a hurry. She had to finish getting supper ready before Mark came home. One thing she had learned in the almost two years they had lived together was that he did not like having to wait for supper. He was an impatient man of routine; not one of those men who became enraged when their routine was broken, but sometimes Amanda wished he would. Instead, he would sulk, and worse, would drink himself into a stupor, which seemed to be happening more frequently. She found this to be infinitely worse.

"I'm hungry," said her five-year-old son, Timmy.

"Go wash your hands, Timmy. Mark should be home soon."

She had just finished setting the table and taking the roast out of the oven when the front door opened and Mark Reynolds called out, "What's for supper?" Without even acknowledging her, he strode into the kitchen and went over to check what was on the stove.

Amanda told him she had made a roast. Mark gave no reply. Even though Amanda had become accustomed to this type of treatment, it still hurt her that he had become less attentive. It had been months since they had made love and even longer since he had demonstrated any affection toward her at all. She thought that even roommates had more interaction than they had recently. Amanda put the rest of the food on the table as Mark quickly washed his hands and then sat down. Only then did she pick up the smell of alcohol on Mark. She started to mention it then thought better, knowing it would only incite denial. Before she and Timmy began to eat, he had finished his food and was leaning back in his chair.

"I thought we'd take a trip," he said.

"What? When?" She questioned incredulously.

"My brother Josh lives up in the mountains. I thought we would visit him."

"What about work?" Amanda asked with an ominous feeling.

"I quit. I couldn't take working for those idiots any longer."

"Great! Now how do you think we'll be able to live?"

"You worry too much. We'll make it okay. I've sold the house and I have some money saved up. Besides, we're not married, so it's not your worry."

Amanda looked at Timmy. "Go up to your room. I'll come up later to say goodnight." She waited until he had left before she spoke. "I can't believe you. You're talking nonsense. There's no way we can survive without an income." She was trying to hold back her tears of frustration and hopelessness. "And what about Timmy starting school?"

"We're going and that's all there is to it," he said through clinched teeth, with his face in hers. "We can enroll Timmy in school when we decide where we are going to stay. You need to spend the next few days getting everything ready so we can leave this weekend."

"I'm not going," she said, trying to keep her emotions in check.

He reached over and grabbed her arm, causing her to grimace with pain.

"Oh, you'll go all right, if for no other reason than for Timmy. You have no money and no place to stay. I don't think you want to go back to living like you were when we met. Now, do as I say and start getting things ready." He pushed back the chair, rose, and walked away.

She stood staring after him, numb with shock. Running her fingers through her hair she held her head in her hands. Her world seemed to be crashing down and disappearing. As she stood up, she began to shiver as quiet sobs caught in her throat. She couldn't help feeling disconnected from the reality of her situation.

Saturday morning the three of them started for the mountains. It was a long, boring trip; made seemingly longer by the single-minded intensity Mark displayed. After hours on the road, they would stop for gas. All restroom breaks were taken during these stops and the only food they bought was out of vending machines. The first few times she and Timmy complained, they suffered his ire and soon learned to keep quiet and simply endure the hardships.

The steady drum of wheels on pavement had a mesmerizing effect on Amanda and she soon found herself drifting off and thinking back to her childhood when her whole life was before her. She had looked forward to the day when she would be able to embrace the wonder, mystery, and thrill of all that the world offered. Finishing high school near the top of her class, she had received a full scholarship to the state university. The first semester she made the Dean's list and was on track to repeat that feat the next term. However, during spring break she met Danny. He was everything she had fantasized about, the proverbial tall, dark and handsome. She was hooked. It started when he asked her to help him study for a history quiz. After that they began meeting for lunch or for an afternoon Coke break. Their relationship soon moved from friendship to passion. She had never had sex before him, but now was a willing participant. She loved him and this physical side of their relationship. It was as if something within her had been liberated, and once released, it could never be put back. She could not get enough of him and this new found pleasure. As a result, her grades began to suffer. She was no longer on the Dean's list and worst of all, discovered that she was pregnant.

"You're what? Are you sure?" Danny asked in disbelief, when she told him.

"Yes. I bought a kit and tried it. It showed positive and then to make sure, I went to a doctor and had the test. Again, the results were positive."

Danny gave her a hateful stare and asked, "Whose is it?"

"Yours." She answered, chagrined, not believing he could ask her such a question.

"I don't believe it. How do you know?"

"I've never been with anyone but you."

"Yeah, sure. Like I'm buying that."

"You know that. I swear it's true!" She struggled to keep from crying.

"Even if you say it is true, what am I supposed to do about it? I hope you don't expect me to marry you or anything dumb like that. After all, I'm still in school. I might be able to help you get rid of it," he said with disgust.

She cringed at the callousness of his words while fighting to hold back her tears. Finally gathering enough courage, she said, "I couldn't do that." She resisted the urge to say it was against her conviction. "I'm going to keep this baby."

"Suit yourself, just don't call me for help." Then he added, "I hope you're not thinking of trying to pin it on me. Remember, I have a number of friends who would be willing to say that you slept with them. Think about it." He made an obscene jester with his middle finger, then turned and walked away.

The next few months were a never-ending descent into despair. Her parents had always been very strict and having no room for forgiveness, disowned her. She took a job as a waitress in a restaurant near the campus. When she was not attending class, she worked waiting tables and only returned to her small rented room to fall into an exhausted sleep. As her pregnancy progressed, she had to drop out of school. It was all she could do to continue waiting tables. Danny failed to return to school the next semester and she never heard from him again.

Timmy was born a normal, healthy child and Amanda continued to work at the restaurant. She alternated taking Timmy to a church day care and having him stay with Mrs. Johnson, an elderly lady who lived in Amanda's apartment building. All of her time was spent between work and taking care of Timmy.

She had been working at the restaurant for around two years when an attractive, tall man with brown eyes and blonde hair came into the restaurant and sat in her area. She could tell by his dress and demeanor that he wasn't the usual blue-collar worker who frequented the place. As she waited on him, her educational background began to show through. They were enamored by the fact that they both seemed out of place. The next day he was back again, and when he learned that she was not married, he came every day after that. Their relationship blossomed from a flirtatious lunch pastime into a more serious need to be with each other in a meaningful, complete relationship.

When Mark found out about Timmy, he was supportive; not like other men who backed away when introduced to him. He brought gifts and took them out to eat and to the movies. For the first time in years Amanda found herself relaxing and actually enjoying life. She also noticed a difference in Timmy. He seemed more active, spending lots of time outdoors and not watching TV as much. One day Mark suggested they move in with him, and after some consideration, Amanda agreed.

The first year was unbelievable. For the first time, she and Timmy could relax; they both found themselves laughing and enjoying life more. Amanda, at Mark's insistence, quit her job and settled into domesticity with abandon. For the first time in her life, she knew real joy and peace.

In recent months she began to notice a subtle change in Mark. When he came home, he seemed to be withdrawn, displaying an anxious, morose disposition. Gone was the old lighthearted demeanor, replaced by a worried, distracted, non-communicative, individual who did not seem to notice if she and Timmy were even there. It all culminated in the flight they were now on.

"Mommy, I'm hungry and I need to go to the bathroom," Timmy said, bringing Amanda back from her thoughts.

Looking over at Mark, Amanda pleaded, "Can we please stop?"

"Oh, all right, I need gas anyway," he replied in a somewhat begrudging tone.

While Mark filled up the car, Amanda gave Timmy a hug as they went inside to use the bathroom and grab a sandwich out of the refrigerator case along with sodas. Mark insisted they hurry and get back in the car, telling them they could eat on the way.

Amanda finally got up the courage to look straight at Mark and ask, "Please tell me what is happening. Why are we in such a hurry?"

Mark's evasive reply was, "I don't want to waste time."

Amanda knew that he was not telling the truth. Until recently, he had always been one who wanted to see some out of the way site, whether it was a natural wonder, or the

41

world's biggest ball of twine. Over the last several months his dreams had become sullen and harsh. Amanda was extremely worried about the reason. It did no good to try to talk with him about it. He would just deny anything was wrong and change the subject.

They drove on until dark and it started to rain. Mark suddenly pulled into a motel with the crazy name of Do Drop Inn.

"I think we can stop here for the night." He pointed next door to a small coffee shop. "We can get a little to eat there and head out first thing in the morning."

Amanda and Timmy were both too tired to express an opinion. They ate a quick bite and all three fell asleep the moment they laid down.

CHAPTER 4

"Josh, it's me," came a familiar voice.

He saw a shimmering shape before him. "Darling is it really you, or am I dreaming?" he asked.

"Both. You are asleep, but I'm as real as you allow. I'm not sure I can explain it, but please, just accept it. I want to be with you, to have you hold me and make love to me. I would give anything if we could," the hazy voice of June said.

"Me too, but I can't see you," Josh replied.

"Just concentrate on what I looked like that last time we were together."

Josh pictured her image from their last goodbye. Suddenly he began to make out her features shimmering in a glowing light. He concentrated on her image and she gradually became clear and distinct. It was as if she were next to him.

Josh cried out "I see you! You are so beautiful. I want to hold you!"

"I know. Me too, but for now this will have to do. Just concentrate on me. Don't let me go. I'm glad Emily is okay. I've visited her before and tried to assure her that everything will be all right. I have to go now, but I will come back if you want me to."

"Please, please, please! I miss you so. I will always love you," he said, with a sob, trying to hold back the tears, wanting desperately to hold on to her.

Later, he awakened, his pillow wet with tears. It seemed so real that he could not shake the feeling that it had been more than just a dream. When he looked over at Emily, he noticed that her covers were askew, as if they had been moved around.

"Get up you two! We need to get going," Mark said in a gruff voice.

"What time is it?" Amanda asked, looking out the window at the still gray morning sky.

"It's almost seven. They have a continental breakfast. I brought some sweet rolls, juice and coffee for you to eat while you're getting dressed."

44

Amanda was half asleep. "Mark, can't we just stay in bed a little longer? Surely a few more minutes won't make that much difference. Timmy is so tired and still asleep."

"I'll wake him up while you take a shower. I want to get away from here before the weather changes. With any luck, we can make it to my brother's place before dark. Now get going!" The tone of Mark's voice showed his impatience.

Having realized the futility of further arguing, Amanda begrudgingly got out of bed.

Josh made breakfast and then went in to wake Emily. She was lying asleep on the disheveled bed, clutching Jocko in both hands. At first, she did not respond to his attempts to wake her. Finally, she opened her eyes, still looking groggy. He studied her for a minute before asking, "Is anything wrong?" She shook her head no and then gave a big yawn.

"Okay sleepyhead, get on up and come to breakfast," Josh said, reaching down to tousle her hair and give her a kiss.

When they sat down to eat, he wanted to ask if anything had happened last night in her dreams; but he decided that it was probably smarter to leave it alone. He got up and walked over to the fireplace, putting another log on the fire. Smiling at Emily, he said, "It sure turned a whole lot colder overnight. I think we should put some more wood up on the porch. As they say in the Boy Scouts, there is nothing like being prepared."

He and Emily, along with the supervision of Rowdy, worked to stack several loads of firewood onto the porch and then fill the log box next to the fireplace. Emily's work was a bit hampered because of her tightly clutching Jocko with one arm.

After finishing, they got into the jeep and Rowdy jumped into the back seat. When Josh moved them to the mountains, he had traded his BMW for the ruggedness and simplicity of a four-wheel drive jeep.

They wound their way to Fairview, a small town nestled in the foothills. It consisted of a gas station, a combination general store, grocery, post office and restaurant. A former motel now served as the school. A

46

few of the rooms there also were used as a medical clinic where a doctor from the nearest town visited on a regular basis every Friday. By far, the prettiest building in town was the small church with a bell steeple. There was a scattering of houses that were inhabited by local residents and a few summer homes for those that liked to fish in the surrounding streams or just to get away from the fast pace of city life. Josh often thought that this was where the term "watching the paint peel" originated. However, it was the very solitude that attracted him. With spring coming on, some of the summer residents had already come back to their homes. Josh pulled the old truck into a parking space in front of Ira Thomas's general store.

"Stay," he ordered Rowdy, as he and Emily went into the store.

"Hi, Josh," said Ira Thomas. "What can I do for you?"

"Ira, we need some supplies and I want to check the mail. Looks like we're going to be in for some bad weather later this week," Josh said.

"Yep, I'd say we're overdue considering how mild the last couple of winters have been. Can't believe how little rain we've gotten."

Josh went over to the area where the Post Office was located. It consisted of one room with mail boxes, a counter with stamps and a few supplies and an area where packages were stored. It was only open M-F from 9-12.

The postmaster, Sam Turner called out to Josh, "Good morning, Mr. Reynolds."

"Good morning, Sam. Looks like we might be in for some bad weather."

"Yes sir," Sam agreed as he handed Josh his mail.

They spent the next half hour gathering up supplies and carrying them to the counter where Ira checked them out. Josh paid the bill and started to leave.

"Just a minute," Ira said, "I have something for Rowdy." He went over to the meat counter and returned with a large bone. "He ought to enjoy this," he said, as he wrapped it up. Then picking up a sucker, he handed it to Emily. "I can't leave you out," he said, with a smile that she returned.

"Thanks, I'm sure they'll enjoy their gifts," Josh said.

"Hold on," Ira said. "There's one more thing I forgot to mention. There was a man in here this morning asking about how to get to your place."

This puzzled Josh. "Did he say what he wanted?"

"Nope."

"What did he look like?"

"Tall, well built with blonde hair that was gray at the temples. He had a woman and a boy with him."

Josh stood with a baffled expression for a moment, then thanked Ira and left.

The sun was already low in the horizon as they started back up the mountain road. Josh was silent, immersed in thought, trying to figure out who might be searching for him. When they pulled into the drive to the cabin, he saw an empty car in front and surmised that whoever it was would be waiting inside, since he never locked the door. Carefully, he opened the door and stepped inside, not knowing what to expect.

CHAPTER 5

"Hello, Brother!"

Josh stared incredulously at the figure before him, momentarily at a loss for words.

"M....Mark?" he finally asked, hesitantly.

Mark laughed. "Yeah, it's me, little brother. Were you expecting someone else?"

"I wasn't expecting anyone. What are you doing here?" Josh asked, with a note of anxiety.

"Relax, brother, I'm just passing through," Mark said, as he looked around the room. "Nice place you have here; really homey. Guess you don't get many visitors up here."

"Not many, we like the freedom," Josh answered, then added, "and quiet." Josh looked at the woman before him. She had thick brown hair and green eyes that reminded him of emerald jewels. Next to her stood a boy around Emily's age. He had sandy colored hair and a smattering of freckles which gave him an appealing Huckleberry Finn type of look.

Mark noticed how Josh was studying Amanda and Timmy. "I'm sorry," he said, "I'm being rude. I should have introduced you. This is my friend Amanda and the young man is her son, Timmy." He saw Emily standing behind Josh. "Hello, Emily," he said, holding out his hand to her. "I'm your Uncle Mark."

Not budging from behind her dad, Emily smiled and waved a hello.

"She doesn't speak since the accident," Josh said, going on to explain about it being psychosomatic and about her always carrying Jocko as a security blanket.

Suddenly, Rowdy came up behind Timmy, and putting his wet cold nose on the back of his leg, startled him, causing him to cry out.

"It's okay. It's just Rowdy," Josh assured him. "He's been in the family since Emily was a baby."

Timmy walked over and began to pet Rowdy, causing Amanda to caution, "Be careful! He might bite."

Emily allayed their fears by hugging Rowdy, eliciting a sloppy kiss.

51

"He would be more likely to bite a steak, but I don't think he would bite anything else," Josh said.

"All the same, be careful," said Amanda, thinking to herself, "Yeah and they said the Titanic was unsinkable, too."

Rowdy licked Timmy's face, evoking a squeal of laughter from him.

"I think you've found a new friend," Josh laughed.

Timmy looked up at his mother, "See, Mommy, he likes me."

Amanda smiled, saying, "He's always wanted a dog."

Masking the fact that he was apprehensive about Mark's strange unannounced visit and also about how his brother looked both haggard and tense, Josh said, "Why don't you all sit down while I put another log on the fire."

They sat around the fire and made small talk. Each time Josh would start to question the reason for their visit, Mark would change the subject, giving Josh an uneasy feeling that this was more than a vacation and that Mark was avoiding telling him something.

"I don't know about you guys, but I'm starting to get hungry," Josh said. Rowdy barked and Josh added with a laugh, "Looks like Rowdy seconds that motion. I'll go and see what I can whip together."

"I'll help." Amanda said.

They went into the kitchen and began to look around. "Don't have a whole lot here. I'm not sure what to fix. I wasn't expecting company."

"Let me see what I can do," said Amanda, as she started to rummage through the shelves. Josh stood watching in amazement as she managed to assemble a delectable meal of diced potatoes, sausage, chopped onion, and scrambled eggs mixed together and served on some flour tortillas she had found. "I noticed a jar of salsa in the refrigerator," she said to Josh. "If you don't mind, open it up and put it on the table."

She scrounged through the drawers and cupboards to find enough plates and utensils for everyone.

"I'm sorry Amanda, I wasn't expecting company, or for you to do all this work," Josh said apologetically.

"It's fine. We should be apologizing to you for barging in unannounced." Then said, with a smile. "Help me set the table while I get some glasses for water and put on some coffee."

They sat down to eat and after taking a few bites, Josh looked at Amanda and exclaimed, "This is really good. I guess I've been eating my own cooking so long I've forgotten what a good cook can do."

The rest of the meal was filled with conversation about what they each had been doing over the past few years. After they finished, Amanda carried the dishes to the kitchen and brought out cups for coffee. Josh volunteered to carry the coffee pot since it was heavy. As the kids went to sit with Rowdy in front of the fire, Mark announced that he was going outside to check on the car.

Amanda began to clear the dishes.

"I'll help you," Josh said, following her into the kitchen with an armload of dishes.

"Thanks, Josh, I appreciate the help."

"No problem," he said, and then added, "So tell me how you and Mark got together? It's none of my business, but I'm curious because you two seem so different."

"He took Timmy and me in and gave us a home. He was very sweet and kind to us. I am extremely grateful." She paused then continued, "I'm worried, something's wrong. He's changed. He's not his usual relaxed self." She went on to explain how he had just announced that they were leaving town in 24 hours with no chance for discussion. "Maybe he'll talk to you," she said, as she looked at Mark with hope in her eyes.

"Maybe so," Josh said knowing that was not likely to happen.

They finished cleaning the kitchen and Amanda asked where everyone would sleep. It was decided that Emily would move in with Josh while Mark, Amanda and Timmy would stay in Emily's bedroom. Amanda went to put the kids to bed while Josh and Rowdy went outside. The night had clouded up and the slight wind had a chill in it.

"Hurry up, boy, so we can go to bed," he said, as he looked around for Mark, wondering if he was sitting in his car. Just as he turned to go back inside, he heard him call.

"Hey, Bro' sure is a nip in the air. Think that storm's getting closer."

"Yeah. I'm planning on going to town in the morning to get some more supplies before it sets in," Josh said, then added, "You are welcome to come along."

"No thanks. I have traveled enough for now. Why don't you take Amanda and the kids?" Josh agreed that would be fine.

They went back into the house and discovered that everyone else had gone to their rooms. Josh said goodnight to Mark as he and Rowdy went to bed finding Emily already fast asleep. He quietly eased into bed and after a few moments felt a sudden warmth wash over him. He was staring into a warm fog when it slowly began to part, revealing a shimmering figure that he quickly realized was June.

"Hello darling," she said in a sing song voice with ethereal quality. "How are you doing with your brother and his friends?"

"Okay," he hesitated then said, "I guess. They just got here."

"Amanda seems nice."

"Yeah, I guess so," he said, then added in a rush, "I miss you so."

"Me too, my darling. But for now, you need to be careful. I don't want anything to happen to you and Emily." Then she added with a laugh, "If it did, I would die!" She suddenly disappeared before he could ask more.

CHAPTER 6

The next morning shone bright and clear with an early spring crispness and gentle breeze to stir the few leaves that had fallen. Josh stretched and carefully tossed back the covers, not wanting to wake Emily, who he noticed had twisted the covers but was still clutching Jocko. He then reached over and scratched Rowdy's head, saying softly, "Hop up boy. Let's go see if we can rustle up some breakfast." Putting on his robe they both headed for the kitchen.

"Good morning," Amanda said. "Would you like a cup of coffee?"

"Thanks, I'm not used to this kind of service," Josh answered with a smile, surprised at how fresh and spry she appeared.

"Thank you," she said, handing him the coffee. "It comes from waiting tables."

"This is really good," Josh exclaimed, walking over to the stove and smelling the bacon that was frying in the pan. Turning back to look at Amanda, he smiled.

Amanda blushed, noticing the intensity of his look, and quickly said, "I'm going to fix pancakes when the kids get up. I'll start yours now."

"Where's Mark?" Josh asked.

"He got up early and said he was going for a walk. He said if he wasn't back soon for us to go on to town without him."

After Amanda placed Josh's food on the table he sat down and began to eat with an appetite greater than usual.

The kids came in rubbing sleep from their eyes. When they saw Josh eating pancakes, they quickly perked up.

"Can we have some?" Timmy asked, then quickly added "please" before Amanda could say something.

Amanda was impressed that he remembered to say "please" and that he had included Emily in his request.

"Boy! That was some breakfast. Those pancakes practically floated off the plate!" Josh exclaimed, as he finished the last sip of his coffee. Feeling content, he leaned back and watched as the kids finished their breakfast.

Amanda placed her hands on her hips and smiled as she replied, "Thank you, kind sir. That's another thing I learned from working at that restaurant."

"I'll do the dishes while you go get ready to go into town. It looks like Mark is not going to make it back. I guess we'll go without him," Josh said, as he got up and rinsed out his cup, then said, "Come on kids, as soon as these dishes are finished let's throw it in the buggy and head for town." Rowdy barked excitedly, knowing from his tone that something was about to happen. Josh laughed, saying, "You too, Rowdy. This time you'll have to ride in the back."

It was a beautiful day, made even prettier by the company with him. They began getting into the jeep with Amanda sitting in Rowdy's old spot next to the passenger window while the kids and Rowdy joyfully piled into the back. The sun shone through Amanda's window, giving her hair an iridescent quality that Josh definitely noticed. The kids were pointing out objects in the small town, and for the first time in a while, Josh noticed that Emily's smile was broader and she seemed much happier. How he longed to again hear her sweet laughter.

When they pulled up in front of the general store, Ira, the owner welcomed them. Josh introduced him to Amanda and Timmy explaining that they were visiting along with his brother, Mark.

Ira welcomed them then said to Josh, "You seem to have become popular all of a sudden."

"What do you mean?" Josh asked.

"There were two men in this morning asking about your brother and you. I think they were going to pay him a visit. I played dumb and didn't tell them anything. Something about them made me think it wasn't any of their business."

Josh thanked him and told him he appreciated his discreteness. He went over to the post office and checked his mailbox, then led the kids over to the soda fountain and made ice cream cones with two scoops of chocolate ice cream for them. They sat side by side at the counter, both beginning to feel more comfortable with one another.

Amanda had reminded Timmy that Emily could not speak and he accepted it with no further questions.

Amanda spent a few minutes putting together a "Jocko care package." Although Emily bathed with him, he was beginning to show wear and tear. Amanda gathered a package of sewing needles and some spools of thread, along with a large sack of cotton balls to replace lost stuffing. Most importantly, was a can of spray disinfectant that Amanda told Emily was "bug spray".

On the way home Josh asked Amanda if she knew who might be looking for Mark. "I don't know." She thought for a moment, then added, "He's been acting very strange lately."

"How do you mean?" Josh asked.

"Just nervous and distracted, like he had a lot on his mind. Quitting his job, selling the house, and leaving so quick. Acting really strange. He said he was overworked and burned out and just needed to make a change. Looking back, it didn't make sense just to pull up stakes like that; and lately he seemed more and more nervous." Gazing into open space, she softly added, "He always seemed so self-assured before."

"When we get back, I'll see if I can get him to tell me if anything is wrong," Josh said, patting her shoulder.

When they arrived back to the cabin, they realized Mark was not there and that his car was gone.

Starring at Josh with a distressed look Amanda said, "I wonder where he is. I hope he's okay."

Amanda walked over to the dining table and picked up a piece of paper that was under a glass on the table and began to read.

"It says he decided to take off for a while to clear his head. He asks us not to worry and he may come back, but don't expect it. We need to get on with our lives and don't worry about him."

With a shaking hand, she handed the note to Josh. "I am worried. None of this is like him. Like I said, he's been acting strange for several weeks." Trying to control her emotions, she added, "I'm also worried about what will happen to Timmy and me if he stays gone."

"Don't worry about that. You both are welcome to stay here as long as necessary." He pulled his cell phone from his pocket and dialed Mark's number to no avail. "Probably has it turned off, figuring we would call. Let's give it a few days and see if it all doesn't work out. Maybe he will quickly work out whatever is bothering him."

"I guess there's nothing we can do anyway. But I'm still very worried," Amanda softly replied.

Josh took the note and placed it in a counter drawer, then turned and said, "I have an idea. Let's eat a quick lunch, then we'll all go down to the creek and do a little fishing."

"That sounds great!" Timmy exclaimed.

A big smile appeared on Emily's face.

Amanda made sandwiches, and after eating, Josh gathered up some fishing supplies and they all headed down to the stream. Josh took a small rod and reel and attached a weight to the end of the line. He showed Timmy how to cast it and then gave it to him to try.

"Are you ready to try it?" Josh asked.

"Yes, oh yes!" Timmy joyfully shouted out.

It took several attempts before he began to get the hang of it. Josh took the weight off of the end, replacing it with a small hook covered with a piece of cheese.

Timmy took the rod and reel and Josh showed him how to cast it into the stream to let the current carry it downstream. The first few times he cast to no avail, but after Josh continued working with him, Timmy finally hooked one. Josh told him to pull on the line to set the hook and keep steady pressure as he reeled it in.

"Be careful." Amanda implored while Rowdy barked his approval.

Josh encouraged Timmy and then grabbed a net to capture the fish.

"Way to go Timmy!" Josh exclaimed, holding up a brook trout. He then took the creel and put some wet grass and the fish in it. Emily, feeling sorry for the fish, bent over to pet it. Timmy went back to fishing until eventually he caught one more.

Soon after Josh said, "I think we better go back. It's getting pretty late."

The first thing Josh did when they got back to the cabin was to get his camera and take a picture of Timmy holding the two fish and grinning from ear to ear. Josh began to clean the fish while Timmy watched intently.

"You and Emily can have the fish for supper," Josh said to Timmy. He then told both kids to go play while he and Amanda started to prepare the food.

"Is something wrong? You have a thoughtful look," Amanda asked.

"No, not really. I was just thinking how little runoff water there was in the stream. This time of year, it should be bank to bank. There wasn't a lot of snow in the high country this last winter, and to make matters worse there hasn't been much rainfall so far this spring." He hesitated and then, in an effort to alleviate any worries she might have, said, "It's still early in the season so we will probably be getting a lot more rain." He looked at her and smiled. "Come on let's call the kids and eat. I want to see Timmy's face as he eats his catch."

CHAPTER 7

The meal had been a great success. Timmy had beamed with pride over having caught the fish. Even Rowdy enjoyed some of the trout. Josh and Amanda ate peanut butter sandwiches since there were only two fish. They had bought a watermelon at Ira's store. Josh cut it so they would each have a slice. He took a triangular piece from the outside middle and bit into it, closing his eyes and, mumbling, "Yum, that is so good."

Amanda gave him a quizzical look.

Josh laughed "I'm sorry. When Mark and I were young our parents would take us to a fruit stand where we got a whole watermelon from a bin filled with ice water. They would cut a triangular plug from the middle of it, to make sure it was okay. Mark and I would fight over it because we both were convinced it was the best piece of all."

Amanda laughed as she took another bite of the delicious melon. After they had all finished eating, she told the kids to go play while she and Josh cleaned up the supper dishes. After finishing, they went into the living room and joined the kids.

As Josh put another log on the fire, he rubbed his hands together. "It still gets a little chilly this time of year after the sun goes down."

"There's something comforting about a fireplace," Amanda said, adding, "That's an attractive box on the mantel."

"Thanks, that contains June's ashes," he said, noticing that she looked sad, and was touched, as she quietly said, "I'm so sorry."

"It's okay, I just had to have her nearby. I write poems as a form of expression. In a college class we were told to find a form of verbal expression we were comfortable with; and I chose writing poetry."

Amanda nodded in understanding.

"Did you read the poem I wrote?" Josh asked, pointing back to the mantel.

Amanda walked over and looked at the framed writing.

> Wonderful thoughts and memories of you,
> like soft summer breezes, flow gently across
> my mind. You have always been there, never
> far from my heart. I rummage through boxes
> of old photographs, like a prospector seeking
> treasure beyond price. Suddenly there you
> are and I want to shout "Eureka", but a tear
> gets in the way. How young we were and
> how much in love. I do not cry for that, rather
> I revel in it, wrapping it around me with an
> understanding that life is a hostage to time
> and timing.
> "Don't cry because something ends, smile
> because it happened." Whenever I think
> of you, I smile. To paraphrase a verse,
> "Do not live in yesterday, it is gone; do
> not look to tomorrow, it may never come:
> live for today, it is enough."
> So darling, if today is all we have, it is

enough. Please know you will be with
me until the end of time and beyond.
I loved you then, I love you now, I will
love you, always.

Josh noticed that Amanda was rubbing her eyes as he reached down and scratched Rowdy's head. They both sat quietly watching the fire.

"Let's put the kids to bed," said Amanda as she got up and turned to Timmy, "Come on big fisherman."

Once the kids were in bed Josh poured them each a glass of wine and they retired to the den where they listened to music on the radio and settled into the two overstuffed chairs in front of the stone fireplace.

"I think the kids, especially Timmy, had a great time," Amanda said.

They sat in silence, sipping their wine and enjoying the flames dancing in the fireplace.

Their reverie was broken when Josh asked, "So, tell me, if you don't mind, how you and my brother met."

Amanda began to tell her story, feeling comfortable enough with him to spare no details about her past.

Josh listened intently, absorbing the emotions in her story.

"What about Mark and you?" he asked.

"He took us in when we needed it most. I'm not sure how much farther I could have gone."

"Did you two marry?" Josh asked.

"No, I would have but he never asked. I was just thankful that Timmy and I had a secure place to stay." Amanda leaned back, stretched, and took another sip of wine.

"Thanks," she said.

"For what," Josh asked quizzically.

"For letting me get all of that off my chest."

They sat back and quietly relaxed for a while.

Josh, noticing Amanda yawning, asked her if she would like more wine. She thanked him, but politely declined saying she was ready for bed. He agreed and they both said good night.

"Hello, my love," came the melodic voice.

"June?" Josh asked with a quivering voice.

"Yes, my darling," she replied." How are you doing?"

"I love you and miss you so," Josh replied, then added, "So does Emily."

"I know, I miss both of you. Some day we will all be together. Until then just remember that I am with you now and forever."

"What do you mean? I want you now," Josh pleaded.

"It is impossible. You must go on with your life. Someday it can change, but until then you must go on and live your life now." Then she added, as she started to fade away, "Amanda can help."

"No, no, don't leave me," he cried.

"Goodbye my love," she whispered, as she faded away.

He awoke covered in sweat, realizing he had been dreaming. Looking over at Emily, he noticed how sprawled out and tangled she was in the sheet. As he went into the bathroom to freshen up, he couldn't help wondering if Emily may have also seen her mother. When he returned, she was awake and, on a whim, he asked her if she saw Mommy. She nodded her head "yes." Not wanting to risk upsetting her, he quickly said, "Let's get dressed and head to breakfast."

He and Emily quickly dressed and headed to the breakfast table, where Amanda and Timmy were already seated.

"Good morning," Amanda said cheerfully. "How did you sleep?"

"Fine," he lied.

"How about some breakfast?" Amanda asked, handing him a cup of coffee and Emily some juice.

They all sat down to breakfast and Josh asked Amanda how she was feeling. He breathed a sigh of relief when she answered, "All right." He did not mention last night even though it played on his mind. He had been visited by June before but to his knowledge this was the first time she had visited Emily. In the back of his mind, he began to wonder if it may have been more than a dream, since they both had seen her. He decided to set his thoughts aside and asked, "Does anyone want to go fishing today?"

Timmy, waving his hand excitedly, hollered "Me, me!"

Josh laughed and said, "Hold on tiger. Let me eat some breakfast and finish my coffee."

Then Amanda proceeded to scramble some eggs along with bacon and toast.

Josh ate hardily, so grateful that Amanda was willing to be the one cooking. After a second cup of coffee he asked, "Is anyone ready to go fishing?"

There was a resounding YES!
They headed out, with Timmy carrying his fishing rod as if it were the most valuable thing ever. As they traveled through the woods, Josh noticed that the vegetation along the way seemed dry. The undergrowth didn't seem to have its usual springiness. When they arrived at the stream, he could tell it was down from its normal volume.

"Can I go fishing right now?" Timmy asked excitedly. While Timmy fished, Emily held Jocko in one hand as she wandered through a clearing filled with wildflowers. Rowdy ran around in circles nearby as she gathered a bunch of the flowers to take back home.

"What's the matter?" Amanda asked, having noticed the troubled expression on Josh's face.

"Oh, nothing major," Josh answered. "I was just noticing how the stream's water level is lower than normal."

"Why are you worried about that? Won't the rain fill them back up?"

"Normally yes, but we haven't had the rains that we usually get, and even more alarming, the winter snowfall was way down this year and we are now going into the time of year when the rain picks up along with the wind. The problem is that this year we haven't had the rain, just the wind and increasing heat."

Nothing more was said as Josh turned back to assist Timmy with his fishing. After being there for a while, Timmy had only caught one tiny trout, so they decided it was time to go back home. Josh convinced Timmy to let the fish go back into the stream. He told him the little guy deserved a chance to grow up.

Once they got home the first thing Josh did was put Emily's flowers in a glass while Amanda prepared lunch.

When they finished eating Josh leaned back and thanked Amanda. He studied her for a moment, thinking how she could use some relief from all the upheaval and tension she had been going through. A sudden thought struck him.

He asked. "How would you like to visit the winery in the valley?"

She let out a squeal of delight, "I think that would be great."

"Awesome, we'll leave in the morning right after breakfast."

The next morning, they hurried through breakfast and Josh told both kids to use the bathroom before they left. They, along with Rowdy, piled into the jeep and headed down the mountain.

Josh could not help but notice the dryness in the air and the warmth of the sun in the cloudless sky. "A nice day, but a little too warm," Amanda said.

"Yeah, it's the start of the dry season," Josh answered, hoping it would not be too long before they got some rain.

CHAPTER 8

They drove through a large, ornate stone arch that marked the beginning of the wine orchard. There were grape bushes as far as they could see on both sides of the road. As they approached the winery office building with its old-world charm, Amanda let out a gasp, "Oh, how beautiful; it looks like a castle."

"Yes," he said with a laugh, "but it has only been around for about twenty years."

They parked and went into the lobby where they registered and purchased tickets for the tour and tasting. Josh told the clerk that Emily always carried her stuffed toy and was assured it would be fine. Their guide, a young girl, led them to an area at the opening of the building where there was a large container. "This is where the grapes are unloaded onto a conveyer belt and 'Pickers' remove as much of the debris as possible. They are washed and then moved to the 'Destemmer-Crusher'. The grapes are crushed and the skin, stems and any other debris that is left is collected at the bottom and the juice is filtered out to the 'fermenter vat' where sugar is added to turn the sugar in the grapes to alcohol." She led them to a cellar where rows of barrels were stacked on their sides. "The liquid is then placed in French oak barrels to mellow and age. The time it is aged depends on the type of wine. When it is ready, it is taken to be bottled." She asked if there were any questions. When they had none, she thanked them and said she would lead them to the tasting area.

As they were heading to the tasting, Josh said, "I do have one question, do you irrigate your grapes, and if so, where does the water come from?"

She laughed, "That's two questions. The grapes are irrigated by a reservoir."

Josh thanked her and she led them to a table where they were given a flight of five wines which had been produced there. Josh and Amanda also were served a platter of cheese and fruit while the kids were served cookies and punch. As each wine was described and sampled, they were encouraged to ask questions. They finished, and on the way out, purchased several bottles of wine.

When they got in the car Josh asked, "Did everyone enjoy themselves?"

Timmy gave a hearty "yeah" while Emily smiled and gave a vigorous head shake.

Amanda reached over and put her hand on his arm, saying, "Thanks." Josh felt as if he had been given a shock.

That evening after dinner, Josh got the kids ready for bed while Amanda cleaned up the kitchen. After the kids were in bed asleep Josh and Amanda retired to the chairs in front of the fireplace. Josh turned on some background music then opened one of the bottles of wine they had purchased that day and poured them each a glass.

Josh lifted his glass, took a swallow, then with a sigh said, "This makes it all worthwhile."

Amanda nodded in agreement and holding up her glass said, "This is the way to end a perfect day." She turned to him and said, "Again, I thank you for taking us."

"It was my pleasure," he said, meaning it.

They continued with small talk until they decided it was time for bed. As they got up, Amanda touched his shoulder with her hand and once again mouthed, "Thank you."

Josh, without thinking, leaned over and gave her a quick kiss on the cheek. When he realized what he had done, he immediately said, "I'm sorry. It was probably the wine."

"Don't be, it was nice," she said, then added, "Besides it was a great ending to a perfect day."

They both stood gazing into each other's eyes, then said goodnight.

Josh got into bed being careful not to wake Emily. He felt mixed emotions as he slowly drifted into sleep.

"Hello," came the voice.

"June?" Josh asked as he tried to make out the shadowy figure.

"Who were you expecting, maybe Amanda?" she replied with a laugh.

"No, no, -- I," his voice trailed off.

"Well, it looks like you are beginning to enjoy yourself around Amanda."

"Yeah, she's nice, but I love you." Josh was shaking his head as he said this.

"It's all right, I know you do; it's a natural occurrence among the living, but you owe it to yourself and those around you to go on with your life. Don't hold back, you need to once again experience the greatest human emotion of all; that of love." She began to fade away.

"No, no, please come back," Josh pleaded.

"Goodbye my love," June whispered as she slowly disappeared.

When Josh woke up, he didn't feel groggy like he usually did after June's appearance during his sleep. As he cleaned up for breakfast, he looked in the mirror and noticed that a smile was on his face. When Amanda brought his coffee to the breakfast table, she put her hand on his shoulder. Her touch felt calm and natural.

Later that day they all went for a walk. As they came upon a small gully that had been washed out by water runoff, Josh helped both of the kids over and then came back to help Amanda. He tightly held her hand to steady her across the water, but once they reached the other side, she did not try to remove her hand from his as they continued walking.

CHAPTER 9

As the days passed, they both became more amorous. What had started out as a touch or a quick kiss began to increase in frequency and intensity. They both looked forward to the evening after the kids had gone to bed and they could be alone. At first, they talked about their past and in general just made gradual conversation as they relaxed from the day. Gradually they began to take on a more serious note as they talked about their hopes and dreams for the future.

As Josh poured each of them a glass of wine he said, "The winery certainly makes a great wine."

"Yes, they do," agreed Amanda. "I like both the wine and the beauty of the place."

Josh got up to turn on the radio. After finding a station that played slow music, he asked, "Would you like to dance, madam?"

"Thank you, kind sir," she said, adding with a coquettish look, "I thought you would never ask."

Josh took her in his arms and they began to sway with the music. They suddenly stopped and stood staring into each other's eyes as though they were seeing one another for the first time. Without saying a word, they embraced and began to kiss passionately. When they finally broke apart, Josh started to apologize. But Amanda shook her head and touched his lips with her finger, "Don't, I wanted it as much as you."

They continued to hold each other as their kisses intensified.

In the future they would look back to remember this moment as the time when their worlds collided and nothing would ever be the same.

As each day flew by, their feelings toward each other continued to grow. It soon became apparent that it was not just a thing of passion, but rather a feeling of true caring that welled up from within. They eventually replaced the old bed with twin beds and moved the kids into one bedroom while they took the other. They could now consummate their lovemaking which seemed so natural. It was not the physical side that they looked forward to, rather it was the intimacy of lying in bed together, reaching over and holding hands as they drifted off to sleep, and waking up in the morning to a kiss. These were truly halcyon days. One morning Josh woke up after having a beautiful dream about the two of them. But when he reached over to touch her, she was not there. He heard noise coming from the kitchen and realized she was fixing breakfast. Suddenly he was consumed with the desire to express his feelings in a poem. He grabbed some paper and began to write.

I lie in Elysium Fields of sleep,
sweet dreams of you wafting,
pleasuring through my mind.

I awake and in that momentary
twilight before consciousness
becomes reality, I reach for you,
but you are not there.

Funny I can still smell your
lingering fragrance on the
pillow, bringing sweet
daydreams to me.

After placing the poem on her pillow where she would
be sure to see it, he walked into the kitchen to find Amanda
giving the kids their cereal.

She turned and said, "Good morning sleepyhead."

The sun, shining through the window, illuminated her
profile, causing him to take in a quick breath. He was
struck by the beauty of the moment and silently thanked
the Lord.

She brought him his coffee and placed her hand on his
shoulder.

"Did you sleep well?" she asked

"Yes, very well," he answered, wanting to tell her he
had been dreaming of her.

After they finished breakfast, Amanda said she was
going to freshen-up and walked into their bedroom. A few
moments later he heard a gasp of breath and she appeared

at the open door. Wiping her eyes, she threw her arms around his neck, giving him a soft tender kiss. He felt a lump in his throat, knowing his poem had touched her.

Later that night as they lay in bed, she said, "I never knew such a feeling of contentment as this. I'll never be able to thank you enough."

Josh leaned over and after a long kiss said, "It is I who should be thanking you. You brought me out of a limbo that I had sunk into. If you hadn't come along, I would still be there. Now I realize that Emily isn't the only thing I have to live for." He reached over and gave her another kiss. "Thank you."

Over the next few days, they enjoyed spending most of their time outside. They had no television, only a radio, so the kids were not tempted to waste long hours sitting in the house staring at a TV screen. Josh worked with Timmy on perfecting his fishing techniques while Emily loved collecting flowers and pebbles. Each of them enjoyed watching the many varieties of birds and animals; even Rowdy would let out a bark of affirmation.

They built a small enclosure out of stones where they placed leftover food for the birds and wildlife. The kids expressed sheer delight while watching the variety of animals that came to eat there.

As Josh observed Emily and Timmy, he said to Amanda, "You know, they never would achieve this type of an educational experience in the city."

After spending most of the day outside, Amanda asked Josh if he would help the kids clean up while she made grilled cheese sandwiches for supper. Both Emily and Timmy were worn out and didn't argue over going to bed. Even Rowdy didn't object, and soon all three were fast asleep. Josh turned the radio to a station that played slow music, as they sat side by side, holding each other's hand and smiling contentedly.

Josh looked at Amanda, saying, "I'm nodding off. Let's get ready for bed."

Josh hurriedly got undressed and stepped into the tub. As he reached up to close the shower curtain, he felt an opposite tug and looked over to see Amanda standing naked before him. He gave a quick gasp, and before he could utter a word, Amanda asked, "Mind if I join you?" That night they drifted off to sleep holding each other's hands.

The next morning, Josh awoke early and lay quietly in bed not wanting to awake Amanda. As he lay there deep in thought he began to realize how quickly things were changing. A feeling of guilt came over him when he realized that June had not been in his thoughts for a number of days. He also thought of the differences between June and Amanda. June was more organized and 'by the book', while Amanda was more spontaneous and easier going. But what it all boiled down to was the fact that one was a sweet memory while the other was a full of life reality. Josh was grateful that he had experienced both in his life. He remembered how lonely and unfulfilled he had felt when he and Emily had moved to their new home in the mountains. Now Amanda and Timmy offered a new beginning, a feeling of completeness, and he felt fulfilled.

During breakfast the kids asked if they could go on a hike. It was a lovely spring day; everything was in bloom and bright sunshine warmed the air.

Something hanging from underneath a limb caught Timmy's eye, and he pointed it out.

"What is that?"

"That's a chrysalis; and the way it's moving I'd say it's about to hatch," Josh replied.

As they sat watching it, something began to emerge. A butterfly appeared and after a few minutes, spread its wings and flew away, much to the delight of the kids. Josh and Amanda had been holding hands. As the butterfly took flight, Josh tightened his grip, feeling a sense of awe. Later that evening he wrote another poem which he left for Amanda to see.

It was a warm, sunny, spring day. We had
gone outside for a walk. As we moved
around, we saw a chrysalis underneath
a leaf on a bush. Looking closer it began
to move and something started to come
out. Suddenly a lovely butterfly
emerged. It rested for a moment,
shaking its wings, then fluttered

off to a new life.

My darling, like that butterfly, we
have each shed our chrysalis to gain
something so much more, a new
beginning, with a love we never
thought possible.

That night their lovemaking was particularly tender
and poignant.

The next morning after breakfast Josh poured the last
of the coffee into his cup, turned on the radio to their
favorite music station, and he and Amanda sat down on
the old chairs in front of the fireplace. They had thought
about going outside but had decided against it because the
wind had picked up speed and was blowing quite strong.
The kids were both content playing with a couple of indoor
games.

Josh reached over and took Amanda's hand in his.

"You know, this is one of my favorite times. Just
sitting back, relaxing, and sharing my thoughts and

feelings with the one I love." He reached down and scratched Rowdy's head, "You too."

Amanda squeezed his hand and they both leaned back, enjoying the sound of the wind outside and the laughter of the kids inside. It was at times such as this that Josh knew there was a God.

Josh had just finished the last of his coffee and was settling back to relax. Suddenly there came a knock on the door. He got up rather reluctantly to head to open it. There were two men standing there. One of them was well-groomed, while the other was more muscular and scruffier looking.

"Yes, can I help you?" Josh asked.

"Mr. Reynolds, we are looking for your brother," the dapper one said.

"May I ask why?" Josh inquired.

"It involves some missing money. Now will you answer me?"

"He's not here. I don't know where he is," Josh replied, and went on to explain. "He showed up a few weeks ago and left his friend and her son here. The next morning, he had left without saying where he was going."

They asked to speak to Amanda. Josh was apprehensive about saying "no." Amanda explained how Mark had taken them in when she was homeless. But she let them know that she had no idea what Mark did. The men asked if Josh would object to their looking around. Not wanting to seem suspicious, he quickly acquiesced. They looked around, then thanking him, handed him a card with a cell phone number on it and told him to call if he thought of anything or if there were any changes.

After they left, Josh turned to Amanda and asked, "I don't know what's going on, do you?"

"No, I just know that Mark has been acting extremely apprehensive lately."

"Well, I hate to say it, but I hope Mark doesn't come back any time soon and bring trouble with him." Josh's tone of voice showed signs of anger as well as worry.

The days moved on in repetition, but the nights were quite a different story. After the kids were in bed, Josh and Amanda would sit in front of the fireplace with a glass of wine and a wonderful contentment that neither had known for way too long a time.

"So, what was your life like growing up?" Josh asked.

"Oh, it was okay. I lived in the country on a small farm. We had very little money and, to a large degree, lived off of the land. We had a vegetable garden, a small orchard where we grew fruit and berries. I liked being outside with the animals we raised: chickens, goats, cows, pigs, even rabbits and some ducks on a small pond. I had to help feed and take care of them. It was both entertaining and educational watching them grow. I spent very little time in extracurricular activities and certainly didn't date. I made good grades in school and received a scholarship to the local community college. Being away from home was a new experience. Until then, I had not dated much at all and certainly never engaged in sexual activity with anyone; and of course, I got pregnant. He deserted me after threating all kinds of things. I dropped out of school and was too ashamed to go home. I tried to make it on my own. I don't think I could have made it without your brother's help."

"What do you want to do someday?" Josh asked.

"I would like to finish college and then work with animals, maybe even to become a veterinarian," she answered. "What about you?"

"I grew up in the city. When I was a kid, I didn't have many friends. I spent a lot of time acting out imaginary scenarios. I played football and tennis, but I wasn't very good at either. While in high school and college I dated very little. I focused on studying and obtained a business degree. It wasn't until I met June that I truly fell in love for the first time.

Amanda reached over and caressed his shoulder, "I'm sorry."

He took her hand saying, "I believe things happen for a reason. If it had happened any other way, we never would have met. I quit trying to figure it all out."

"Me too, I'm just glad that your brother brought Timmy and me here." They kissed, then sat holding hands, quietly reflecting on how their journeys had brought the two of them together. Eventually, they grew tired and decided to go to bed.

CHAPTER 10

The next morning when Amanda awoke, she discovered that Josh was not in the bed. She called out and he answered from the kitchen.

"Just a minute; I'm bringing the coffee," he said.

He came in carrying a tray with coffee and sweet rolls on it. Setting the tray down and leaning over, he gave her a kiss.

"Good morning, Sweetheart," he said, kissing her once again.

"My, aren't you the spry one," she spoke. "You usually lie here half asleep while I make the coffee."

"I know, but I have something special this morning for you to see," he said, handing her a sheet of paper. "I got up early and wrote another poem that I want you to read."

"Sure! You know I love your poems!"

Is this real or only an illusion, I ask
myself. Surely, I am not entitled to
this much happiness. Yet when I hold
you, or kiss you, or just talk to
you, the answer comes with incredible
clarity.
It is real and maybe everything else is
illusion.
My love for you is the one certainty in a
world full of ambiguity. And if this earthly
orb we occupy should disappear, my love
would continue through empty time and
space.

When she finished, she looked up at him and said, "Oh darling, that is lovely. I feel the same way."

After they hugged and kissed Josh handed her another folded sheet of paper, saying "I have one more thing for you to see."

Giving him a quizzable look, she took the paper and opened it. There were only two words printed on it. She sucked in her breath and let the paper fall.

MARRY ME

"Yes, oh yes, my darling!" She jumped out of bed to embrace him.

After a while Amanda said with a laugh, "I think the coffee has gotten cold. Let's go tell the kids."

Over the next few days Josh and Amanda made the plans for their wedding. The kids felt important since they were both going to be ring bearers. It was decided that Josh would keep his old wedding ring while Amanda would use the one June had worn.

The wedding would be held at the church in town even though there was a possibility that they would be the only ones there.

On the day of the wedding the whole family dressed up. Josh wore a sports coat and Amanda a sundress. Timmy protested having to wear slacks instead of shorts or jeans, while Emily became very excited to wear a pretty dress. The day was sunny, dry and windy as they drove down the mountain road to the town. The church had a chapel with an altar, and an old upright piano where an elderly lady sat to play. To Josh's surprise, all of the church's benches were filled with parishioners, including Ira and his wife Alice.

The kids stood waiting at the altar with Emily holding Jocko, and when the piano began to play "Here Comes the Bride," Josh and Amanda started their walk down the aisle. Amanda carried a bouquet of wild flowers that Emily had picked. For the ceremony the preacher read the traditional marriage service. When he pronounced Josh and Amanda husband and wife they kissed and Josh whispered, "You are my everything." The preacher, Charles Abbott, offered his congratulations and wished them well. Josh thanked him and slipped him a fifty-dollar bill. The other parishioners clustered around them with congratulations and introductions.

Once they were outside Josh asked the kids if they wanted to go to Ira's for ice cream, eliciting a big 'yippee' from Timmy and a big smile and an affirmative head shake from Emily.

Even though Ira's was only a few blocks from the Church, the wind was blowing so strong, that they decided to drive.

Ira congratulated them when they came in and then asked the kids if they would like a shake instead of the usual ice cream scoop. This created a loud "yippee" and head shake.

"Boy, that wind is really blowing out there," Josh stated.

Ira nodded his head in agreement, "Yeah, it's been that way off and on for several days. I had planned on cooking some hot dogs and hamburgers outside on the charcoal grill for all of us, but it is just too windy. I'm sorry, but I'll need to make them in here."

Josh thanked him and said that would be fine; but in the back of his mind the weather worried him.

After they ate, Josh bought Amanda a windbreaker and a scarf as a wedding present. He then went across the room to the post office to check the mail.

"Congratulations," the postmaster Sam said. "I wish you both a wonderful life."

After thanking Ira for their food, they headed back to the cabin. On the way home Josh reached over and squeezed Amanda's hand.

"I was going to write a poem about this, but I'm so full of emotions that I can't find words strong or meaningful enough to express my feelings, and how incredibly blessed I am!"

She looked at him, "I have never known this much happiness and contentment. My darling, I love you more than life itself." Squeezing his hand, she added, "For the first time I can remember, thanks to you, I am at peace with myself."

They came across a truck parked by a stream. It had a tank in its bed with water flowing out into the stream. Josh pulled over and they watched as it finished its flow. He asked one of the men what was happening and was told that they were releasing trout fingerlings. Timmy wanted to go fishing and catch some of them until he was shown their tiny size.

"Don't worry, we'll let them grow, then catch them later," Josh said, giving him a reassuring hug.

Josh looked around and then asked, "Everything looks pretty dry and the stream is low, will the fingerlings be all right?"

The man in charge said that they would be okay as long as the stream ran and did not become polluted by debris and growth. Josh thanked him and said how much they appreciated all of their hard work.

After thinking about the dryness, Josh decided it might be a good idea to remove all the brush and debris from around the cabin. The family spent the next few days creating a fire 'buffer zone' by clearing the area around the cabin and grounds for approximately thirty yards. Some small trees were cut down and others were trimmed, especially around their base. The rest of the time was spent entertaining the kids, while teaching them about nature and life, but making sure that both they and Rowdy had plenty of play time.

Josh and Amanda discussed how they would like to become more of a family with the kids. Josh decided that he and Timmy, along with Rowdy, would camp out in the yard for a night just to spend a little time alone and get to know each other better. Amanda thought that was a great idea and said that she and Emily would spend time cooking, decorating and playing games. When the kids were asked what they thought, there was an enthusiastic response.

Josh and Timmy drug out an old tent Josh had kept and the two of them put it up in the clearing they had created in front of the house. They placed a sleeping bag for each of them inside. Once they had finished Timmy asked, "Mr. Reynolds, what about food?"

Josh told him, "We'll build a small fire pit and roast some hotdogs and marshmallows I brought along. By the way, don't call me Mr. Reynolds, from now on just call me Dad."

Josh looked over at Timmy and saw a timid yet warm smile on his face as he nodded his head in the affirmative. Josh handed Timmy a shovel and they dug a small pit. When they had finished, Josh asked Timmy to help him gather up some small stones.

Timmy asked, holding up a stone, "What are these for Mr., I mean, Dad?"

Josh explained that they were for making a fire break around the pit's perimeter. After they finished placing the stones, they gathered small branches of wood and Timmy helped Josh look around for two long, thin branches growing on a tree. These green branches would be used to skewer their hot dogs. Timmy asked if they were going to cook any hot dogs for Rowdy. Josh replied, "Sure, you can cook a couple for him because he'll be hungry too."

Later that evening as they sat roasting marshmallows and relaxing around the fire Josh asked Timmy what he might like to do when he grew up. Timmy said without hesitation, "I'm gonna be a park ranger." Josh smiled as he patted him on the shoulder. Looking Timmy straight in the eyes he said, "You will be an awesome ranger." Timmy had a sweet smile on his face. Josh noticed what a good-looking kid he was with such light brown eyes and sandy curly hair.

After Timmy yawned a couple of times Josh decided it was time for them to go to bed. As they lay in their sleeping bags with Rowdy at their feet Josh said, "Goodnight, Timmy." The reply he heard was soft but clear. "Good night, Dad."

Josh fell asleep that night with a warm feeling inside. He now had a son.

Earlier that same day Amanda had taken Emily to a huge blackberry bush at the edge of the clearing and let her help pick the berries to make a pie. When they got back to the cabin Emily was allowed to help in every step of the baking process. Once the pie was placed in the oven they headed back outside and walked hand and hand to a nearby field of wildflowers. Amanda held a basket and told Emily she could pick any flowers she wanted.

"When we get back to the cabin, we'll put them in a vase. It will be your own beautiful creation. Emily tucked Jocko tightly under her left arm and ran from flower to flower, pointing to the ones she wanted in the basket. Watching Emily gleefully run around the field Amanda felt a tinge of sadness at not being able to hear the joyful sound of laughter coming from this precious little child. She said a quick prayer that someday soon she might again

106

be able to speak. After the basket was filled with an array of beautiful color, they headed home to use the arrangement to decorate the kitchen table.

The smell of the baking pie was wonderful. Emily wanted a piece as soon as it came out of the oven, but Amanda said they would wait until after dinner. There was still more work to be done. Emily went with Amanda to help pick fresh vegetables from their small garden. They used them to make a great salad to go with their dinner. After they ate Amanda placed two small plates with slices of pie on the table, smiled and said to Emily, "Here's the pie made with the berries that you helped me pick. You are such a great helper." Emily felt her cheeks grow warm and beamed with pride as she admired the pie sitting on the plate in front of her. It was, of course, the most delicious pie she had ever tasted.

Later that night as Amanda helped Emily with her bath, she noticed Jocko sitting on the edge of the tub and said to Emily, "Jocko is getting pretty dirty, but it would be bad if he got in the tub with you. Is it okay with you if I wipe his face a little with this wet wash cloth?" Emily smiled and nodded her head. It made her happy to see how gently Amanda rubbed his face.

It had been a fun yet tiring day when Amanda, Emily and Jocko headed to bed. When Amanda leaned over to kiss Emily's forehead and whisper goodnight to her, Emily smiled and reached her hand over to rub Amanda's arm, causing her heart to skip a beat.

Josh and Amanda's nights were full of entertaining themselves with not only the pleasures of the body, but also with thoughts and plans about their future. Living remotely, they would need to home school the children and to also buy a laptop for their use. Still, they felt that the benefits of their surroundings far outweighed the negative aspects.

CHAPTER 11

Several days later they decided to take a drive up the mountain.

"I know we both keep saying it, but it really looks dry," Amanda said, with a worried look.

"It's that time of the year when there is little moisture," Josh ventured. "What bothers me more than the lack of rain is the wind. It seems stronger and lasts longer than is normal for this period of time. I saw a sign at Ira's from the Forest Service saying, 'No burning, no open fires, subject to a fine and possible arrest.' Everyone really needs to be extremely careful not to allow any kind of open flame that could rapidly turn into a full-blown forest fire."

Josh noticed a scenic overlook and quickly pulled in. He parked next to a couple seated underneath an awning which was attached to a small travel trailer being pulled by a pickup.

"Hi, a little warm today," an elderly man said.

"Yes, it is," Josh said with a nod of affirmation.

"I'm Ed," the man said. Then pointing to the woman seated next to him, added, "This is my wife, Iris."

She waved and said, "Hello."

"You folks live around here?" Ed asked.

Josh told him they did and that they were just out for a drive. He reached for Ed's hand while saying, "Glad to meet you. I'm Josh and this is my wife, Amanda." He felt his heart swell as he realized how good it felt to say that. "These are our kids, Timmy and Emily."

"Hello," Ed said then asked, "Is it usually this dry and windy around here?"

"This is the dry season. It will last a few more months," Josh answered. "Just have to be really careful with fire."

"Yeah," Ed replied. "I didn't light one. We wanted to cook out but it was just too dry and windy."

They chatted for a while longer. Iris offered the kids some of her homemade baked cookies, which they eagerly accepted. Josh and Amanda thanked them, and saying their goodbyes, told them to enjoy the rest of their trip and left.

As they drove up the mountain road, the kids were thrilled by all the wildlife they continued to spot. They were particularly excited when they saw an eagle perched in a tree which suddenly took flight as they drove close. Rowdy stood in the back seat with his head out the window, letting the wind blow over him. He kept barking with excitement and wagging his tail to display his happiness.

They noticed a scenic pullout and decided to stop for their picnic. The cooler with the sandwiches and drinks was carried to a picnic table with benches.

As they sat and ate, the kids had lots of fun feeding pieces of bread and crackers to the squirrels, chipmunks, and a variety of birds. Rowdy barked with joy as he began chasing them.

After finishing their meal, they continued up the road until it ended at a turnaround. Josh looked at the GPS and said, "Well, this seems to be the end of any road." He pointed to a trail that headed around the side of the mountain. "It looks like that foot trail goes to the other side and connects with a different road that leads down the other side of the mountain and back into town. It all makes a big loop, making it the start and finish. We can only get to that road by foot from here, so we'll have to turn around and head back down."

Once they returned to the cabin, Josh and Amanda spent the next few days discussing what the future held for them, especially concerning the kids.

"We are going to have to do something about the kids and their education," Josh said. "It's too far to try to take them to school, especially in the winter."

"You're right. Do you have any ideas?" Amanda asked.

"Maybe, I've been doing some research and it seems there is something called 'Hot spotting', where a laptop is connected to a cell phone."

"Will that work up here?"

"Should be fine since we get cell service."

"Can you use the phone at the same time?" Amanda asked quizzically.

"I am assured you can." Josh said, trying to sound confident about something he knew nothing about. "Looks like our kids are growing up." Then as an afterthought, added, "Maybe me too."

She leaned over and gave him a kiss, "That makes two of us."

A few days later Josh told Amanda that he had ordered the computer equipment for the kids' home schooling.

"It will take about a week before it gets here. How would you and the kids like to go on an overnight camping trip? It so happens that I have an old tent that I brought with me, just in case we had to have a place to stay in an emergency if something happened to the cabin."

"It would be good for the kids to spend some time outdoors with nature," Amanda stated.

"You can help me get some things together," Josh said. "We'll need bug spray, the first aid kit, a saw and a shovel."

"And toilet paper!" Amanda added emphatically.

"Once the sun goes down it gets cold. We need to take a jacket for everyone. I have two sleeping bags that you and I can use and we'll take a blanket for the kids," said Josh as he became more excited.

Amanda said she would pack a change of clothes for everyone and bathing suits, just in case they came across a stream.

"Great," Josh said, "As dry as it is, just make sure nothing needs to be cooked; we will only be able to have a very small fire. And don't forget to bring some food for Rowdy."

When they told the kids, Emily hugged Jocko in delight and Timmy hollered, "Yippee!"

They left the next morning and worked their way across the side of the mountain on some old logging roads, until they came to a campsite where a small waterfall fed the stream. It was an isolated spot and because it was during the week, they were the only ones there. The kids were begging to put on their bathing suits and go play in the stream by the waterfall. Josh told them that they would have to help unload the tent and set up camp first. He knew that they would not be of much help, but it would be a good lesson in responsibility.

After the Jeep was unloaded and the tent set up, Josh took the shovel and cleaned any debris from an area. He then dug a small fire pit, setting the dirt in a pile, then lined the rim with some stones. They would sit around it that night and perhaps roast some marshmallows and hot dogs in it, and nothing else. When they were finished, the dirt which he planned to remove along with the stone, would then be used to fill the pit back in and be carefully wetted down with water.

Once the chores were finished, they all changed into bathing suits. The kids ran and jumped into the water, hollering from the shock of the cold mountain stream. Emily was careful to hold Jocko up high so he would not get wet or cold. Rowdy barked with excitement then splashed around in sheer joy, wetting them all. The plan to swim did not last long, because that mountain water was icy cold. The kids soon hopped out shivering, ready for a warm towel.

After Josh suggested that they change their clothes so they could go on a hike, everyone hurriedly put on jeans, long sleeved shirts and boots. A makeshift pouch was created for Emily to carry Jocko on her back. Josh gathered a canteen of water, a machete, his phone and a pole he had made from a tree limb. He also had a small air horn, just in case they needed to scare something away. They followed a trail through the growth, seeing many birds and animals; squirrels, racoons, porcupines, chipmunks, even a beaver that was moving in the distance by a pond. There were all kinds of birds, even another eagle.

They saw a snake and both kids were frightened. Timmy let out a yelp as Emily immediately clutched Jocko tighter to her chest. As the snake quickly slithered away, Josh told them that it was okay. "It's all right; just a harmless snake, not poisonous. You can tell by the shape of the head. He went on to draw figures in the dirt. Most poisonous snakes have triangular shaped heads. The non-poisonous ones have an oval shaped one. The main thing is just to leave them alone. They will try to stay clear of us, because they are just as afraid of us as we are of them."

They hiked further on and saw a myriad of plants and animals as they marveled at being surrounded by the beauty and wonder of nature. Josh made a sweeping gesture saying, "God is not just up in the sky, but all around us." Eventually, everyone became tired and the decision was made to return to camp.

CHAPTER 12

When they returned, Timmy said he was hungry and Emily signaled her feelings by rubbing her stomach. Josh took the kids to gather wood for a small fire. He also cut four small green tree branches to use as skewers to cook the hot dogs and marshmallows.

Amanda mentioned to Josh that Timmy kept saying that he was starving.

"Yes," said Josh, "It's amazing how being out in nature brings on the appetite."

They finally filled up, sat back and relaxed, enjoying their surroundings. Josh opened a bottle of wine and poured a glass for Amanda and himself. The sun was going down and it was starting to become cool. Josh put another log on the fire and they all moved in closer to it. There was a full moon and no clouds to hide the beauty of the shimmering sky.

"Look at the moon." Josh said, pointing upward. "It is lighting up the whole sky." He looked at Timmy saying, "Maybe someday you will go there."

Timmy just stared at it, not saying anything, deep in thought. Emily tugged on Josh's sleeve and pointed at herself and Jocko.

"Okay," Josh laughed. "You can go too."

He turned to Amanda, making a sweeping gesture towards the sky. "I can't believe that God hasn't created other life since we are only a speck in a vast universe of which just a fraction of it is visible. I wonder if on another world somewhere out there, a family is sitting together around a fire, just like us, gazing up at the stars in their sky. It's hard to believe that we are just a microcosm of what's out there." He thought for a moment, then taking another sip of wine, continued, "What if the whole universe is only an atom, a spec in a bigger one, and it in turn, is in an even bigger one. Maybe black holes are gateways to them." He took another sip of wine, then reached over to squeeze Amanda's hand, saying, "One thing I know for certain, I don't care how many universes there are as long as I am with you."

It was beginning to turn cold and the kids were becoming tired and sleepy. Amanda suggested that they all go to bed, for which Josh was grateful. After carefully extinguishing the fire, he helped Amanda arrange the sleeping bags and blankets in the tent. Timmy, Emily and Rowdy all fell asleep almost instantly. Josh and Amanda huddled under the covers, exchanging kisses as Amanda propped herself up on one shoulder as she looked into Josh's eyes and said, "I love you, no matter what universe we are in." They fell fast asleep, holding hands.

The next morning, they all got up early. After a quick breakfast, Josh asked them if they would like to go swimming before they left; but remembering that freezing water, Emily immediately started shaking her head and clutching Jocko closely for protection. Timmy hollered out, "No way! Brrr!" They decided to go ahead and leave and began loading everything into the car. The air was cold, but the bright sunshine felt good.

The first few days back at the cabin were quiet. Timmy asked Josh if he could go fishing. Josh agreed and the two of them went to the stream, while Amanda and Emily stayed behind to make brownies.

The next day, Josh received a phone call from the postmaster Sam informing him that there were a couple of packages for him at the post office. Josh thanked him, then loaded everyone into the jeep, and headed to Ira's. When they arrived, Josh told Timmy and Emily that they could have a milk shake while Amanda picked up a few groceries and supplies. Josh went over to the post office where Sam Turner handed him several packages.

Sam smiled as he said, "Good morning, Josh."

"Morning, Sam," Josh replied, then added, "Try to stay cool and keep from blowing away."

Sam laughed. "I don't think I'll be flying any kites; they'd be flying me."

Josh was happy to see that the packages containing the laptop and accessories had arrived. He carried them over to the counter where the kids were finishing their shakes.

121

"Good morning, Ira. I was just wondering if you had seen those two men again."

"No sir, just that one time," Ira replied.

After Josh paid for the kids' shakes and the supplies Amanda had gathered up, he wished Ira a good day and they left.

When they arrived back at the cabin Josh unpacked the laptop along with the printer and accessories. After several phone calls he finally had it working. The kids were both excited and fascinated at having a computer of their own. Both Josh and Amanda told them emphatically that it was primarily for their schooling. If they wanted to use it for anything else, they had to ask for permission first. They checked out the kindergarten program along with a few other ones. Emily liked the books, Timmy the puzzles, and both liked the games. They were not allowed to use the printer since paper was scarce. Ira sold the paper, but was often out of it.

Amanda set the hours they had to study on the computer; two hours in the morning and two in the afternoon. She said that if they wanted to play on it, they had two hours after supper. She thought that might help make them sleepy.

Josh used the computer to check the news, weather, and other information programs to help keep in touch with the outside world. He decided to look up information on an ancestor his parents had mentioned. Finding it interesting, he printed it out and showed it to Amanda.

Adam Reynolds, age 100 in 1835, was among the first taxpayers of Greene County. He was married to Susan Johnson and later after her death, to Elizabeth Carpenter. Between them they had 10 children. His farm was located in both Greene and Washington Counties. Adam was captured by French and Indians in 1758 at Fort Painter, Virginia. His mother and five of his sisters were also captured. His father, George Reynolds, was killed during the raid. Revolutionary War Pension Application S. 1923, gives a further account of Adam Reynolds' capture. He states in his

pension application that on one occasion he
joined General George Washington's army
on the red banks of the Delaware River and at
another time at the Schuylkill River.
He served five tours of duty and was at the
Battle of King's Mountain.

"Wow, what an adventure," Amanda said.

"Yeah," Josh replied. "Sometimes life is more interesting and exciting than any movie or a good novel. After all, it's these experiences that create our knowledge and understanding of life, behavior and the world around us."

The kids were into their studies and playtime on the computer. The wind was wildly blowing.

That combined with the heat and dryness, made it uncomfortable outside, and creating no temptation to venture forth.

CHAPTER 13

Barry Miller looked at his wife.

"If it's okay, I think we'll pull in here for the night," he said, pointing to a little roadside park.

"It'll be fine," Susan Miller answered. "As long as we are out of this blasted wind."

They pulled into the clearing and Barry got out, saying to Susan, "With this wind I don't think we'll try to pitch a tent."

Susan agreed, "Yeah, it would probably pitch us."

He laughed, then said, "I'll just move the front of the van into the wind and move the supplies from the back up to the front and fold down the rear seat. We can sleep there."

His wife agreed and they went to work preparing it.

Barry said, "I'll start a small fire at the back end. The van will protect it from the wind."

He unloaded a cooler that contained beer, a few soft drinks and cream for cereal and coffee. He set up a small grill and placed some charcoal in it.

"I think I'll have a beer before we start supper."

"A drink sounds like a good idea to me," Susan agreed, pulling out a bottle of wine.

"This is the life," Barry said, as he opened another beer and settled back in the folding aluminum lawn chair. After his third beer and her half bottle of wine, they started supper. He placed several hot links on the grill they had brought while Susan put out paper plates and plastic silverware along with some condiments. They placed a rock on each plate to keep them from blowing away.

They finished their supper, threw the "dinner dishes" into the fire, and then each poured another drink.

"It would be a wonderful evening if this blasted wind would go away," Barry said.

"Yeah, and a little moisture would be nice. My skin feels like an old shoe," added Susan, rubbing her arm.

Barry studied the sky. "At least the full moon and the clear sky with all the stars makes it look like a crown full of jewels."

After a while longer they decided to go to bed. Barry placed a metal tray over the glowing coals in the grill and they quickly fell asleep in the rear of the van.

The next morning Barry awoke, still groggy from a combination of too much to drink and having slept in the back of a van instead of on a mattress. He removed the metal tray from the grill, replacing it with a metal rack and adding more charcoal to start a new fire. He brewed a pot of coffee and they settled back to drink several cups and ate some powdered doughnuts.

After they finished, Barry asked Susan if she was ready to go, to which she enthusiastically answered, "Yes"! Barry dumped the paper plates, eating utensils and cups in a trash bag to take with them then dug a small pit and placed the coals in it and threw some dirt over them.

They packed up everything and after looking around one more time, they got in the van and drove away. The area where there had been a fire was no longer protected from the wind by the van. A sudden gust blew over the area where the fire had been, lifting a small smoldering charcoal ember, depositing it in some dry grass at the edge of the clearing, where it began to grow in intensity.

Josh, Amanda and the kids, wanting to beat the heat, started early on their morning walk. Josh noticed that the grass was withering and turning brown. Many of the plants were dying from the dryness and they cracked, breaking apart when stepped on. The stream which should be flowing bank to bank was now barely a trickle. There were dead fish floating belly up, having become trapped in ponds that had been cut off of the main stream.

When they returned home, Josh reminded them to be careful and watch their use of water.

"I'm afraid that the water level in the well will get too low to use."

Water had become a precious commodity, only being used in a small amount to wash dishes. Clothes were washed in what water was still flowing in the stream and very little soap. Bathing consisted of a sponge bath with a wet wash cloth. On their weekly trip into town, Amanda pointed out how dreary everything had become.

At the grocery store they bought what they needed, including ten one-gallon jugs of water for drinking and cooking. When they went to check out Ira said, "Sure are a lot of people buying water, afraid their cistern and wells are going to run out."

On their way out, they overheard a couple complaining about the weather having caused them to leave the mountain after only one day.

For the last several evenings, after sunset the heat dissipated somewhat, causing the wind to die down. They would all sit outside and relax under a bright canopy of stars. Occasionally they would see a shooting star and the kids would clap with joy, eliciting a loud bark from Rowdy. Something gnawed at Josh, but he put it aside, choosing instead to enjoy the evening. Along that line, he gave Amanda another poem he had written.

I lie asleep, as sweet thoughts of the
two of us, flow like a warm, gentle
breeze, through my mind, filling it with
the promise of what is yet to come.
I ask myself what did I do to deserve
this much happiness?
I awake and realize you are there,
beside me and it is not a dream but
sweet reality, that wraps itself around
us, spilling over with a wonderful
promise of more dreams, yet to come.

That night their love making was particularly poignant.

*The ember landed in a clump of dry grass where it
rested, simmering, gaining strength. When it had become
alive with new found energy, it chose to spread its wings
and try another area. It allowed the next gust of wind to
lift it up, and riding the thermals, it came to a large pile of
brush and more dried grass. Deciding it looked promising
it came down, full of renewed energy. It began to flex its*

muscle and before long fulfilled its lifelong dream as it
burst into a glorious flame.

After sunset, the family had moved outside to enjoy the somewhat cooler air. The kids and Rowdy spent time chasing lightning bugs and playing hide and seek.

"This limited use of water reminds me somewhat of my hiking and backpacking trips," Josh said to Amanda. "I remember one where several friends and I went on a narrow gage train that traveled up a mountain to a small town, where it spent several hours letting the passengers' shop and look around, before it came back down. The train was crowded when we got on with our gear and it was hard to find a seat. We ended up sitting apart with our packs in our laps. Halfway up the mountain there was a small open area where the train stopped if anyone wanted to get off. The five of us did, and we watched the train pull away before fastening our packs and heading along the trail. After an hour or so, we came to a spot where we decided to set up camp. It was there that we stayed for four days backpacking in the mountains, before going back to the track to signal the train we were ready to be picked up. This time, after not having bathed in four days, when we got on the crowed train it was like the parting of the Red Sea," he said with a laugh. "We got any seat we wanted!"

CHAPTER 14

The next morning Josh went outside to breathe in the cooler morning air before it heated up and dried out as the day progressed. He soon came back inside with a worried look on his face. Amanda noticed it and asked him what was wrong.

"I smell smoke; step outside and see if you do too."

Amanda went to the door and ventured out. After a few minutes she came back inside.

"You're right," she said to Josh, "I certainly smell it. What do you think could be causing it?"

"I don't know," he said, "but I don't think whatever is causing it is good."

The kids were hungry, so while Amanda fixed them breakfast and fed Rowdy, Josh called Ira at his store in the town.

"I'm smelling smoke," he said. Then asked, "What do you think could be causing it?"

"Don't know," Ira replied, "I heard that there might be a small fire at a rest stop not far from your area. I'll let you know if I hear anything," Ira reassured him.

Josh thanked him and hung up.

As the day progressed, more smoke began to accumulate. At one point the radio news station Josh had tuned in to interrupted their program to say that a fire reported earlier in Josh's area was gaining in intensity. As if by some telepathy, Ira called to say that the fire was getting larger and was located between town and where Josh's cabin was.

"You might want to think about an evacuation plan, just in case you need one," Ira said, then added, "If you have to, you could go up the mountain and come down the other side. The only problem is that the road from your place stops at a small park before you reach the crest. You would have to follow a foot trail to the top and then walk down the other side that loops back to town."

Josh thanked him, then added, "Hopefully the Forest Service or the National Guard would be able to evacuate us, if necessary."

"Probably," Ira replied, then added, "Just remember, your electricity will stop, and even though you have solar, the smoke can be thick enough to cut out the amount of light needed to create ample power."

As Josh thanked him, Ira promised to keep in touch.

That evening at supper, Josh told Amanda that they should start gathering up items to take with them in case evacuation became necessary.

"That smoke is getting thicker and a slight shift in the wind could blow it this way. I'm not sure that we could be evacuated in time if that happened. Let's eat a quick meal, get the kids settled down and get ready in case we have to leave first thing in the morning. We have to be very limited in what we take in the jeep. Remember, we may have to abandon it if the road is impassable and we will have to move on foot. We'll take as much as we can, but again, if we have to leave here, we'll only be able to take the bare minimum." They began to gather the supplies. Amanda was grateful to stay busy, feeling as though she might panic if she had time to dwell on what could happen to them.

Josh said, "We may be going on foot and need jeans and long-sleeved cotton shirts, no synthetics. They would burn easily. Get hiking boots and thick socks. We may have to travel through hot ashes."

Amanda volunteered to gather up the bottled water they acquired and get the food. Josh pointed out that they should bring only such items as dry cereal, fruit, energy bars, cookies and whatever did not require openers or eating utensils.

Josh shouted, "We need some gauze pads, tape and bandages, also some aspirin and that tube of burn ointment we have." Then as an afterthought, said, "Might put in several rolls of toilet paper, and we need to fully charge our cell phones along with the flashlights, before the generator quits."

They finished packing and gathered everything into the jeep, knowing the next day would be harrowing. Josh decided they should try to get a few hours of rest because fires could slow down a little at night, due to the slightly lower temperature.

The alarm went off at five that morning. The smell of smoke was significantly higher, causing Josh's noise to burn and his eyes to water. The smoke and heat were increasing in intensity, causing the cabin's emergency generator to switch to fuel driven mode. Josh knew it would soon quit altogether and they had to hurry. He looked outside and was greeted with a surreal landscape. Clouds of billowing smoke and tongues of fire danced across the hills and into the sky. Bolts of dry lightning added to the already hellish scene.

After rapidly checking the car and supplies he joined Amanda, the kids and Rowdy, to quickly eat some of the perishable food that they would have to leave behind. When they had finished, everyone took turns quickly using the toilet. Then they, along with Rowdy, jumped into the jeep and after Josh took a picture of the surreal scene around them, took off leaving all their hopes and dreams behind.

They headed up the mountain road, keeping ahead of the fire. As daylight arrived, eerie clouds of gray black smoke billowed around them. Amanda noticed that the kids were becoming agitated and invited them to sing some of their songs with her. Josh thought how ironic it was that except for the fire, it almost felt as though they were on a pleasant outing. The kids were fascinated by the wildlife, including the multitude of birds that they saw, all moving in the same direction to escape the fire.

Josh tried several times to reach Ira on the cell phone, but the mountains blocked the signal. Not wanting to run the battery down, he waited until they reached a high spot where he finally connected with Ira who expressed his joy that they were okay. He told Josh that due to the dryness and wind the fire had quickly turned into a major event. There had been very little time for the fire fighters to organize and to plan any rescue. Ira agreed with Josh that his plain to go over the mountain top to the other side made the most sense. Josh thanked him and explained that he did not want to run his cell phone battery down so he was going to hang up. Ira wished them well and said to call him if they needed help. Josh hung up and immediately was overcome with a feeling that he and his family were now all alone.

They reached an area where a large granite outcropping forced the road to reverse directions turning them back down the mountain, towards the fire. Josh soon came to an area where flames were erupting on both sides of the road. This, along with the thick swirls of smoke, formed a tunnel over the road. Josh stared at the scene before him and felt that he was about to go through what could be the entrance to hell. He told everyone to cover their face with a cloth. To protect and calm the kids, he told them to take Rowdy and lie down in the floor board with their jackets over them. Amanda lowered the seat and curled up. Josh, saying a quick prayer, told Amanda he loved her, and drove the jeep into the vortex before them.

The intense heat along with the blinding smoke and flying embers was choking. Even though it was almost impossible to see, Josh knew he had to keep going and could not stop, no matter what. The only way to tell where they were heading required watching the road's edge and following it. Suddenly there came a loud crashing sound and the jeep shook as a large tree feel across the road, barely missing them. Just as Josh felt as though he could go no further, the road turned back up the mountain. They took a deep breath, grateful to be granted a brief respite from the smoke and heat.

Incredibly the jeep was still drivable. The whole vehicle was covered with soot. Unfortunately, the windshield wiper blades were unusable, making it hard to see.

CHAPTER 15

They continued up the mountain until they reached the spot where the road ended at a small park. The fire and smoke were still heading their way but not as intense as before, because the vegetation was less dense in the higher location.

Josh told the kids to hurry and use the park's restroom while he let Rowdy out for a few moments. Josh tried reaching Ira, but to no avail. Turning to Amanda, he said, "We need to hurry. We've got to get walking up the trail so we can cross over to the other side. Hopefully the rock face will stop or at least slow down the fire's advance. Let's pack the food, water and whatever else we might need into our backpacks and the kids' knapsacks. We can even use Rowdy's pouch." They quickly loaded the packs and Josh took Amanda into his arms, saying, "I want you to know that no matter what happens, having you in my life has made it all worthwhile."

After a brief yet intense kiss, they quickly strapped on their packs and headed up the trail. At first the journey was easy, and in other circumstances would have been pleasant. But as they progressed, the path became steeper and narrower, forcing them to move into a single file. Josh and Rowdy went first, followed by Emily, Timmy, then Amanda.

It was now midafternoon and the kids were quickly reaching the point of exhaustion. Josh began to worry about how much further they could continue when suddenly a niche that was cut into the rock wall on the trail appeared. He decided it was the only area where they could rest that would offer any protection from the elements. Each of them unrolled their sleeping bags in order to avoid sitting on the hard, cold, rocky ground.

Amanda opened a couple of cans of Vienna Sausage and a box of crackers. While that was being readied, Josh looked around and gathered up a few handfuls of dry leaves along with twigs and small limbs on the floor of the alcove. He soon had a small fire started that served more for comfort than warmth. "How ironic," he thought with a laugh, "that we are creating the very thing we are trying to escape."

They all sat around the fire and ate their meager meal. Rowdy was given a handful of dry dog food. The children remained very quiet and obedient, realizing how very serious the situation was. Once they finished eating, the kids quickly crawled into their sleeping bags and along with Rowdy, were soon fast asleep.

Josh and Amanda sat huddled together appreciating the fire's meager warmth. Light from the forest fire below them flickered, dancing across the sky. Amanda hugged Josh and softly said, "You know anywhere else, you would have to pay a premium to enjoy a light show such as this."

Josh nodded in agreement, then said, "I was wondering how many ancient people including kids and dogs, may have spent nights just like this in an alcove's rock wall." Amanda's eyes sparkled with their own fire as she spoke, "We are in the very same spot, and even though we are under stress, we have a home to go to. Think how those nomads felt with no end in sight."

They put their arms around each other, enjoying the warmth and closeness provided by these unusual circumstances. They huddled together for several more minutes; but with each of them knowing how tomorrow would be such a daunting challenge, they quickly hugged and kissed, saying a quick prayer before crawling into their sleeping bags.

After a few hours of sleep, the family hurriedly ate an energy bar and drank some powdered protein drink mixed with water. After feeding Rowdy they quickly packed their sleeping bags and headed out. The fire was still raging below but was actually slowing in the higher altitude due to the thinning vegetation. As they moved closer to the peek the trail was becoming steeper, narrower and rockier, forcing them to travel single file as they had the day before. The fire continued to slow down as it worked its way up the mountainside. Josh knew they had no choice but to keep going until they reached an area where the terrain was open enough to allow rescue.

An unseen eagle perching on a ledge suddenly took flight, startling them all. Rowdy barked and Emily dropped Jocko. As she quickly reached down to retrieve him from where he rested on the narrow trail edge, she lost her footing on the loose rock and slipped over the edge's rim.

Amanda screamed, Timmy stood in shock, Josh cried out and Rowdy barked. Fearing the worst, Josh moved quickly to the edge. Looking over, he was relieved to see that Emily had landed on a small bush that protruded from the mountainside below. Josh lay down and tried to reach her, but she was just out of his reach. She was holding Jacko in one hand and the bush with the other. Emily's weight was causing the bush to pull away from the rock's face. Josh realized it was just a matter of minutes before it would break away from the rock. He did not have time to improvise a rescue device so he lay down and reached for her but she was just out of his grasp.

"Let go of Jocko and reach up and grab my hand," he cried out.

Emily shook her head. She would not let go of Jocko! The movement of her head caused the bush to shake.

"Please sweetheart," Josh pleaded, as he strained to reach her.

Suddenly a shimmering image they both recognized as June's, appeared to both of them.

"Let Jocko go!"

Again, Emily shook her head, refusing.

In a more pleading voice, June's image said, *"Please darling, do it for Daddy and for Me. I love you and want you to do this! Let Jocko Go."*

Emily suddenly released Jacko, and as he fell away, she reached up and grasped Josh's hand. He pulled her up at the very moment the bush broke loose and fell into the vast chasm below. Josh stood up and Emily put her arms around him, with tears in her eyes. Turning her face toward his, she cried out, stuttering in a raspy voice, "D-d-d-daddy."

A tear ran down Josh's face as he was overcome with emotion. Amanda and Timmy encircled them with their arms as Rowdy barked. They all began to laugh and cry at the same time. Josh looked up at the sky and repeated over and over, "Thank you."

146

Hugging Emily even more tightly he softly whispered into her ear, "I love you, my precious little girl."

CHAPTER 16

Carefully gathering around on the ledge, they all took a welcome break to hug, kiss, and laugh as Emily chattered away, overwhelmed with joy at her ability to finally speak again. They continued huddled together until Josh said, "We better get going. I would like to reach the top in time to find a flatter, open area where it might be possible to have a helicopter come pick us up."

They started up the trail with Emily continuing her constant prattle as Rowdy echoed with excited barks. Their joy and relief to finally reach the top soon turned to disappointment when Josh discovered that it was too rocky and windy for a safe pickup. After discussing the situation with Amanda, they decided to start down the other side to look for a more suitable place to make contact and to arrange a pickup. The new trail was still rocky and narrow, but fortunately did not require the physical demand of more climbing. However, loose rocks were still a threat and they all needed to be extremely cautious.

Emily, exercising her new-found vocal ability, could now ask questions and express opinions on a variety of sights and sounds that she noticed along the way. Josh merely laughed, ever grateful that she now had the desire and capability to do so.

As they descended down the trail, they saw several aircraft flying over the fire area behind them, releasing their load of chemicals. After traveling over an hour, they came to a wide spot that was fairly level and not as rocky. There were even a few trees nearby that were a welcome sight; not because they were needed for their shade or protection, but rather for the comfort they offered against the stark terrain they had just experienced.

Josh turned his phone back on, and after several attempts, he managed to reach Ira who was excited and relieved to hear they were all okay. He quickly assured Josh that the store, and for the most part, everything around the town was unharmed. Josh then told him where they were and asked him if he could reach out to whoever was in charge of rescue to see if they could help. Ira said he would start immediately and promised to call back as soon as he knew something.

Daylight was rapidly disappearing as Josh and Amanda gathered their packs together and removed the sleeping bags along with some food. They took a couple of tarps and using some fallen tree branches improvised a lean-to which they could sleep under, not so much for protection but rather for a sense of togetherness in this vast open area.

Josh wanted to build a fire but was too afraid to, so they all huddled together while eating a bit more of their meager rations; making sure that Rowdy was also fed. Josh knew that they only had enough food for one more day. The fire raging behind them gave an eerie, dancing glow to their surroundings. After finishing their meal, Josh said that he wanted to say a prayer and he had everyone join hands. He thanked the Lord for Emily's recovery and bringing them this far. For the first time since regaining her voice, Emily began singing. Josh became choked up to hear that lovely sound once more. They all joined together and continued singing with Emily leading the way, enjoying every word even if mispronounced.

Soon the children's heads were nodding and Amanda said it was time to call it a day. Rowdy curled up at the foot of the sleeping bags. Josh and Amanda decided to sleep on each side with the two kids in the middle so they could be of comfort to them and help keep them warm

Josh stayed awake until he was certain the other three were fast asleep. He lay there thinking that despite all that had happened in the last few days he could relax and smile. He thanked God for the magnitude of blessings he had right there within that rustic little lean-to.

Josh awoke to see the first rays of sun filtering through the smoke. He roused the others, telling them to hurry and get ready. They rolled up the sleeping bags and tarps and tied them to their backpacks. Then they sat down, along with Rowdy, to finish off what was the last of their rations. When they finished, they put the empty containers into their packs and Josh used Amanda's phone to call Ira because his was dead. After several tries, he reached Ira and told him what had happened and where they were. Ira told him that the military was operating helicopter rescue missions and assured Josh that he had contacted them and arranged a pickup. Josh thanked him and to ease his tension, light-heartedly told Ira to keep the cheeseburgers ready.

Josh and Amanda sat on their packs enjoying a few moments of peace as they waited to be picked up. The kids and Rowdy were scurrying around, picking up pine cones, broken limbs and interesting rocks. Every few minutes Emily would run over to them to chatter away about some treasure she had found. Josh looked over at Amanda and said with a smile, "She's become quite a chatter-box, but I am thanking God for it."

Before long they heard the whup-whup sound of a helicopter as it flew over them, finally landing at the clearing's edge. The kids stood transfixed as they watched it land while Rowdy hid behind Josh's legs and barked. A man jumped out and ran over to them. He asked if everyone was okay, and after receiving assurance that they were, grabbed the bags and told them to follow him to the helicopter. Josh picked up a nervous Rowdy and carried him. Once they settled in and the helicopter lifted off Timmy and Emily stared out the window in silent fascination as they flew over the countryside while Rowdy huddled next to Josh's feet.

Josh looked in awe as they flew around the area where the fire was still raging and then back around over the already burnt part. He felt both sadness and fascination at the powerful destruction the fire had created. As he looked out the window a tanker aircraft flew by in the distance releasing its contents of chemicals on the fire.

Josh turned to the crewman sitting with them and asked, "Are they making any headway in containing the fire?"

"Some," the crewman answered. "They have it about thirty percent contained and are managing to slow its advance."

"Is the town still okay?" Josh asked.

The crewman answered, "Yeah, it looks like it will be spared." Josh breathed a sigh of relief and thanked the Lord.

Soon the town came into view and they landed in an open area at its edge where a camp had been set up. Josh picked up Rowdy as they all exited the helicopter. What a welcoming relief it was to see Ira there to meet them.

With a huge smile on his face, he hugged Josh and said, "Sorry no cheeseburger, but I am really glad to see you guys."

"Believe me, too many times I was doubtful that I would ever see you or this place again," Josh answered with a catch in his voice.

Ira hugged Amanda, and as he turned to hug the kids he heard a sweet little voice asking, "Can we have some ice cream?" He quickly jerked back his head in shocked amazement, turning to Josh with a questioning look on his face. As Josh gave a quick explanation of what had happened to Emily, Ira, overcome with emotion, turned his head away from Josh and broke down in tears.

CHAPTER 17

With great excitement and a little anxiety, they all piled into Ira's pickup and were taken to their new home. It was a two-bedroom, one bath older home that Ira owned and had often rented out to tourists; however, he insisted that they stay for free. He had even left them some nonperishable food, clothing and toiletries. Unfortunately, there was no electricity at this time. They were all worn out from the trauma and lack of sleep they had endured over the last few days and were asleep in a matter of moments.

On awakening the next morning, they quickly dressed and headed to Ira's store. When Josh entered, he was astonished to notice that food shelves and hardware areas were both empty. Ira told him that because people were afraid of not having food or supplies, they had quickly stripped them bare.

Timmy and Emily asked Ira if they could have their usual ice cream and Ira had to tell them he did not have any, but promised a double dip when he did. After Josh said a blessing, the kids settled for peanut butter and jelly on crackers while Josh and Amanda ate canned tuna fish. Rowdy was given some dry dog food and water. They all drank apple juice because it did not require refrigeration. Josh and Amanda agreed it was one of the best meals they had ever eaten. Ira continued to refuse payment. Over the next several days Josh helped Ira and his wife Alice clean out the refrigerator and freezer of all the spoiled food. Once the electricity was restored, Josh worked with Ira making repairs around the store and other properties that Ira owned, including the one where they were staying. Amanda worked helping some of the homeowners reorganize while Timmy and Emily spent time in a summer school which had been started by the local church mainly to keep the kids busy. Rowdy spent his free time in the fenced backyard chasing squirrels.

One morning after they had been told it would be several more days before they could go back to check out their cabin, Amanda went into the bathroom to freshen up.

When she looked into the mirror, she saw that there was a poem taped to it.

> I look up at the heavenly firmament of the
> night and see an endless array of shimmering
> light, the music of the spheres. I open my heart
> and feel surging through me, the music of my
> love, playing but one perfect song, undiminished
> in its consistency; it is your song. For you are
> the music that fuels my heart and feeds my soul.

With tears in her eyes, she went straight to Josh. As he started to speak Amanda put her finger to his lips to silence him. She then gave him a kiss, not of passion but of incredible love, wonder and joy.

Several trucks of food and supplies finally arrived at Ira's store. Surrounding churches and charities were now able to bring needy families help. The Forest Service had been able to open the road going up the mountain for those who lived there. Josh borrowed Ira's pickup, and leaving the kids and Rowdy behind with Ira, he and Amanda drove up the mountain. Josh had to drive slowly and stay alert to avoid the large amount of debris still scattered on the road. They passed a burned-out trailer.

"That looks like the one those nice people we met were in," Josh said.

"I hope they are all right," Amanda replied with a sick feeling in her stomach.

The landscape was blackened and the smell of burnt wood filled the air. They finally reached the cabin and were relieved to see that it was still standing. The metal roof was intact and the stones and logs were all in place although blackened in some spots by the fire.

As they exited the truck Josh put his arm around Amanda, holding her close while they observed what had once been green and alive, but was now replaced by a fire scarred and dead image of itself.

On closer inspection they noticed that the intense heat had caused several windows to crack. When they went inside everything seemed intact; however, the whole place was covered with ashes and the intense smell of woodsmoke, and none of the utilities worked.

Josh went outside and walked over to the edge of the forest, grateful that by cutting it back they had created a firebreak around the house. Something caught his eye. On closer inspection he saw a small green plant growing up through the debris of burnt leaves and limbs. He thought, "This is how it is with life; one thing dies but another takes its place and life goes on."

After gathering up their clothes, the kids' laptop, and some utilities, they headed back to their temporary home.

Josh volunteered to help clean up debris left on the road and parks while Amanda, Timmy and Emily continued their work. Josh went to Ira's to see if he needed any help. Ira thanked him saying everything was under control. He handed Josh an envelope addressed to him saying, "Charlie Jones brought this to me. He said a stranger had asked him to give it me so that I could deliver it to you." Josh thanked Ira as he opened the envelope.

Hey Bro,

I hope all is going well and that
Amanda and the kids are doing
okay. I want you to know I appreciate
all that you have done for me. I won't
be seeing you for a long time but please
know I love all of you and wish only
the best.

Love, Mark

Josh gave the letter to Amanda. After she had read it he asked her what she thought. She said that she was touched by what he wrote, but it still did not answer questions about what was taking place in his life. There was no return address so they could only pray that he was doing okay.

CHAPTER 18

A few days later Josh asked Amanda if she and the kids would like to take a ride. He suggested they go to visit the winery which he hoped had been spared a lot of damage from the fire because of the fact that it was located in the valley. They all shouted with glee at the opportunity to enjoy a break. As they neared the winery, they noticed that the vines looked wilted and the facade in front was broken and lay on the ground. Fortunately, the metal building housing the winery itself seemed intact. They were greeted by the same young girl who had helped them before. Josh mentioned that the grapevines looked wilted and was told that even though the fire missed them, the wind and drought had done a lot of harm. In addition, the irrigation system was damaged and they were waiting for parts to fix it.

"What about the wine?" Josh asked.

"We have what is bottled and what is making, but it doesn't look good for a new harvest."

Josh nodded sadly and said, "I hope everything turns out okay." When he asked her if they could buy some wine she enthusiastically replied, "You bet, they all survived in good shape because they were stored in the cellar."

After purchasing the wine Josh again thanked her and wished them well. Amanda gave her a warm hug of reassurance.

When they arrived back at the house everyone was hungry. Once Amanda finished preparing their meal and they had all sat down, Josh brought out one of the wines they had purchased. As he poured a glass for Amanda and himself, he took her hand and proposed a toast.

Lifting his glass, he said, "Lord, we are so grateful for the fact that we are with one another and enjoying life, no matter what it brings."

It wasn't long before they received a notice that the electricity was now working at the cabin. They went to Ira's, thanked him for all of his help, and then began gathering up their belongings to head back up the mountain.

When they arrived, the first thing they did was to turn on the water pump so they could begin cleaning up. A canister vacuum was used to remove ashes which covered every surface. The refrigerator was plugged in and once again filled with food. Broken windows were boarded up and the bathroom plumbing checked.

After several hours of hard work, they went outside to relax and enjoy the fresh air. They were amazed by the rapid growth which displayed the effort nature was making to resurrect itself. There were butterflies and other insects along with an occasional bird. Josh was distracted by Rowdy's barking. When he went to see what was causing it there was a small bird hopping around on the ground. He pulled Rowdy away and on closer inspection saw it had a damaged wing. Later that night he handed Amanda a poem he had written.

> I saw a bird with a damaged wing
> Hopping around on the ground, trying
> to fly.
> As I watched it struggle, I was

amazed that it was still singing its

bird song.

It was then that I realized that like

that bird so must we; for God wants

us to keep his song on our lips and in

our hearts no matter what life brings us.

She smiled, put her arms around him and giving him a kiss, whispered in his ear, "I love you."

Over a short period of time, with Ira's help and connections, they were able to have the window glass replaced along with the broken solar panels on the roof. Ira loaned them his chainsaw to cut down some of the worst burned trees and bushes. Amanda took an old pan and made a birdbath by placing it on a structure made from stones and small tree branches. They dug up some of the colorful wild flowers to create a small bed on each side of the front door.

One night as they sat down to dinner, Josh gave thanks to the Lord for all their blessings then added a request for a little rain.

Their days were filled with hard work completing the restoration and cleanup. At one point Josh and Timmy walked over to the stream where they discovered that it was now just a trickle. No fish or other aquatic life was visible. With a distraught look Timmy asked, "Will we be able to go fishing again?" Josh smiled, patted him on the shoulder and assured him that the fish would come back when it rained.

With their food and supplies running low they decided to spend the weekend in town. On their way in they noticed that all the fallen trees and brush along the road had been removed. When they arrived at the house Amanda let out a delighted gasp when she discovered that Ira had painted the house Verdewhite with attractive grey shutters.

As soon as Joshed stopped the car, they all quickly piled out. When they let Rowdy out, he bolted in front of them, eager to run around the backyard to reacquaint himself with the squirrels. Emily stood on the front porch, quickly running inside as soon as Josh unlocked the door. With a happy squeal she hollered out, "The walls are a different color from before." Once inside they opened up the windows to air it out and then discovered that the interior had been refinished. There was a new stove and refrigerator while the bathroom had been remodeled with a new tub-shower combo, commode and sink.

They hurried to finish and then headed to Ira's to thank him for everything.

Ira's face lit up when they walked in. "Hey guys, it's a pleasure to see you."

Josh and Amanda, both thanked him for all he had done. When Ira asked the kids if they would like some ice cream, they both answered with a loud cry of "Yes! Please!" Amanda smiled when she heard them both say "please." She told them to be on good behavior as she looked around the store for a few things she needed to buy.

"How are things going?" Josh asked.

"Pretty good," Ira assured him. "Everything is getting back to normal. Food and necessities are now available. The doctor's office has opened for their once-a-week visit and the school is being made ready for this fall."

Nodding his head, Ira looked up at Josh and added, "Your kids are going to like it."

They talked for a while longer when Ira suddenly asked Josh if they would like to go over to church with him and Alice the next day. Josh answered that they would look forward to it.

That next morning after breakfast they let Rowdy out and headed to the church. Ira and Alice greeted them and led them over to chat with Pastor Abbott and his wife Janet who asked Timmy and Emily if they would like to go to the play area in back and meet the other kids. They both were excited and followed her to a fenced area that surrounded a small building where there were several swings, a seesaw and a merry-go-round. Timmy and Emily both were happy as they joined the handful of kids who were already playing there.

Josh and Amanda followed Ira and Alice inside to a pew. The preacher announced that they were visiting and the whole congregation warmly welcomed them back. Then the pianist Ms. Morgan played the old familiar hymn "Rock of Ages." All present gleefully joined in singing it loud and clear. Pastor Abbott stood, and moving to the stand that served as a pulpit began to give a sermon that truly touched Josh. One thing he took note of was that when we die all of our infirmities, disfigurements, pain, and poverty will be gone, because as spirits, everyone is equal. When he finished, they sang another hymn, and after the benediction, the congregation went into the lobby where, along with the children, all enjoyed a bring-a-dish meal. Josh and Amanda thanked everyone, saying they looked forward to coming back. Timmy and Emily both were excited to hear that. They had already decided that they loved this church.

CHAPTER 19

After spending the night in town, they headed back to the cabin, each with a warm feeling inside because of the new friends they had made. As they pulled up to the cabin, Josh noticed that the relaxed comfort he always enjoyed upon arriving there was not the same. He thought it was probably that the feeling of being a part of the community they had experienced in town was now missing. The whole family had felt the friendship and honest caring of those people at church.

Josh unloaded the car while Amanda put everything away. Later, when Josh went outside to water the flowers in front, the kids also went out to fill the feeders for the birds and squirrels. Josh noticed how the new growth that had sprouted was now beginning to wilt, and he said a prayer, once more asking the Lord for some rain.

They all worked the rest of the afternoon cleaning up and making what repairs they could to get everything into shape. Amanda with the help of Emily, planted several herbs she had brought from town. Josh and Timmy collected small broken limbs and branches, placing them in a pile. Rowdy enjoyed his usual pastime of chasing birds and squirrels. They worked for a couple of hours until they were all tired, even Rowdy who had given up on the chase and fallen asleep.

Everyone was tired from the day and as soon as dinner was over the kids and Rowdy went to bed. After cleaning up the dinner dishes Amanda poured each of them a glass of wine and sat down by the fireplace where Josh had started a small fire. The moon, surrounded by twinkling stars, shone big and bright through the window as they relaxed and sipped their wine. Josh looked at the stars and marveled at the vastness of God's universe. Filled with emotion, he reached over to give Amanda's hand a gentle squeeze. She squeezed his hand back and whispered, "I love you." They finished the wine and decided to go to bed, both falling asleep almost as soon as their heads reached their pillows.

The next morning Josh was awakened by sun shining through the window onto his face. Seeing that Amanda was still asleep. he carefully arose and headed into the kitchen to make coffee. As he sat down enjoying the morning and the beautiful sunshine that spilled into the room, Amanda came in, stretched, gave him a kiss, then went to pour her coffee. She suddenly gave a little squeal after seeing that her cup contained a piece of paper rolled up inside it. She opened it and began reading.

> Like some mischievous animal, the
> sun's early morning rays come
> creeping over, under and around
> the slits in our bedroom blinds.
> How I wish I could shoo them
> away. They interfere with my
> dreams of you.

She came over, bent down and giving him a kiss quietly said, "You are my dream come true."

Later that day they decided to drive up the mountain to the road's end. When they came upon their burned-out jeep, they were all filled with a cold horror, remembering what they had gone through. Josh suggested they all join hands and pause for a moment of silence.

After they arrived back at the cabin, Josh and Amanda discussed how they were both feeling a sense of loss and they made the decision to return to town. Josh was surprised by the serenity he felt upon arrival at the house in town. He looked over at Amanda and noticed a contented smile on her face. They quickly unloaded the car and headed to Ira's. After arriving, the kids headed to the soda fountain for ice cream. As soon as Amanda noticed Ira, she felt the urge to give him a hug. Holding back tears of emotion, she did just that. This precious man had seemed even closer than family to them. In order to keep from bursting into tears she quickly excused herself, leaving to gather the food and supplies. After she left, Josh and Ira sat down with a cup of coffee as Josh brought Ira up to speed on the status of the cabin and the mountain roads.

"What about here?" Josh asked.

"Everything is going well. Life is pretty much back to normal," Ira answered. Then, taking another sip of coffee, he asked, "How are you and the family doing?"

Josh filled him in on all that had been happening.

They continued talking until Amanda and the kids showed up. As Josh got up to leave, he thanked Ira for all of his help and said that they would like to go back to church on Sunday. Ira happily responded that both he and Alice would love to attend with them.

The next day when they arrived at the church Ira and Alice were already there waiting for them. After warm greetings, they all went inside to the small narthex where coffee and juice along with sweet rolls were waiting. Timmy and Emily went to be with the other children who were rapidly becoming their friends.

Pastor Abbott acknowledged Josh and Amanda, saying it was a pleasure to see them and the children again and that he hoped they would continue to come back. Josh was so impressed with that morning's sermon, especially the closing prayer. He later requested a copy of it:

Oh Lord help us to remember that you
are not just in the sky above but in
everything we say and do.

Oh Lord it is you who lights our path
through all the storms that life brings.
Let us open our hearts so we may see
you in all we say and do.

Oh Lord we give thanks to you for
bringing us together to share the
wonder, joy, heartbreak and love
that we experience in this world you
created. May our lives reflect your
love and caring in all we say and do.

After church the family headed back up to the cabin. Upon arrival Josh noted that the wind had subsided somewhat and that there were more clouds in the sky. With school starting soon, Josh and Amanda spent some time making plans for the kids. There was a van that would come and pick them up along with several other children; however, in inclement weather they would have to home school.

They were splitting time between the cabin and the house in town where they purchased food, supplies and attended church. When school began, they spent each weekday at the cabin. Both Josh and Amanda would accompany Timmy and Emily to the road, waiting with them for the school van to arrive. Both kids enjoyed school where they made closer friendships and learned new subjects.

Josh noticed that the strong wind along with the heat, had subsided and more clouds filled the sky.

Their days at the cabin were filled with the kids going to and from school and then studying at nights. During the day Josh and Amanda made themselves busy around the cabin and enjoyed the time they had to be alone. They continued spending weekends in town relaxing with their new friends and going to church.

One day while the kids were in school the sky darkened and Josh could feel a dampness in the air. A cluster of dark clouds began moving their way. Excited by the prospect of rain Josh pulled his chair to the window.

Ahead of the advancing storm, the leaves began swirling around like snowflakes. He could see the rain moving toward him. Suddenly he felt a hand on his shoulder. Turning, he saw Amanda standing behind him, warming his heart with her smile. She asked him to pull the other chair over closer while she brought them a bottle of wine and two glasses. After she poured each a glass of wine, they settled back to watch nature's spectacular show.

The next morning Josh presented Amanda with a poem he had written.

> I sit here in my chair looking out the window,
> watching as the outside darkens and the room
> begins to chill. The wind is moving through
> the trees, shaking their limbs, causing their
> leaves to fall like snow, as it gains strength.
> Soon the storm will be here.
> Suddenly everything brightens. I ask myself

"Is the storm over?" Then I realize it is not the storm but you entering the room. For my darling, you bring new warmth and light to me.

She gave him a hug and a kiss saying, "I am so lucky to have you." He answered, "No darling we are blessed to have found each other, just when all hope and desire for life had disappeared."

The rain had not lasted for very long but they both hoped that it was a portent of what was to come. The next several weeks were filled with the same scenario of school, weekends in town, and church.

One day Amanda told Josh that after the kids left for school on the van that she would like for them to go into town because she wanted to see the doctor. Josh had a worried look as he asked if there was a problem. She smiled and assured him it was just a "female thing" and not serious.

The next day Josh dropped Amanda off at the doctor's and went to visit Ira. When her visit was over, they headed back to the cabin, arriving before the kids came back from school. Josh and Amanda walked out to the road to wait for the van. When they arrived, Josh noticed how both were laughing and appeared to be excited. They all hugged one another; Josh tousled Timmy's hair while Amanda leaned over and gave Emily a kiss. Rowdy barked as he ran in circles.

After returning to the cabin the kids sat down to do their homework while Josh worked on a couple of projects and Amanda began preparing dinner. When Josh finished his work, he went into the kitchen to ask Amanda if she needed some help. As he looked at the table something caught his eye. "What is that for?" he asked, quizzically pointing at an extra plate.

"I thought I would just check out how it is going to look," Amanda responded.

He hesitated, thought a bit, then asked, "You mean, are you saying that you're --pregnant?" Then taking a deep breath, he began asking a litany of questions, "How, where, when is it due, what sex is it"? Then, looking lovingly at her face he paused to ask, "How are you?"

With a laugh she said, "Hold on tiger! To answer all your questions; first, I think you know the how and where. Don't yet know the sex, but we'll know in around seven months. The baby and I are doing fine." Smiling, she looked lovingly at him, then began hugging and kissing him, whispering, "Thank you."

The kids were called to dinner, but nothing was said to them about the baby at that point. After the meal, they cleaned the kitchen and gave the kids a hug as they put them to bed. Josh kissed Amanda as he patted her belly, shaking his head and saying, "I still can't believe it." Putting his arm around Amanda, they went over to the chairs in front of the fireplace. The nights were becoming cooler so Josh built a small fire for them to sit in front of while Amanda brought out the last bottle of wine from the winery that they had been saving for a special occasion; they both agreed that this was it. Holding hands, they smiled peacefully while watching the flames dancing in the fireplace.

Josh took a sip of wine and said, "We have a lot to talk about."

Amanda, making a silent sign with her finger to her lip softly said, "Not tonight."

They continued to hold hands as they silently enjoyed the tranquility of the moment. When the last sip of wine was finished, they decided to go to bed. As they got up and embraced each other, Josh bent down giving Amanda's abdomen a kiss. "Sleep tight, both of you." That night their lovemaking was even more meaningful.

The next morning Amanda went to the bathroom to wash her face and saw a sheet of paper taped to the mirror.

My darling the two of us have known
pain and heartache in our past lives and
relationships. When we met that was changed
forever. Now the two of us have become
blended into one so that we have a glorious
and all-consuming love.
Out of that love we have fused together,
creating a unique new being to experience all
the emotions life brings.

A tear rolled down her cheek as she set the poem in a safe place.

CHAPTER 20

That afternoon when the kids came home from school Amanda and Josh said that they had something great to tell them. With Timmy and Emily both seated, Amanda knelt down, taking the hand of each, and told them about the baby. They both sat there quietly, letting the info soak in and then they both started talking rapidly at once, asking questions. First and foremost, they wanted to know if it was a boy or a girl. Amanda said that it was too soon to know that. The baby was still too tiny. Timmy said he hoped it was a boy so they could play games together while Emily hoped for a girl.

Josh put his arms around them and said, "I know you will have fun together. Let's just pray that it is healthy, no matter which it is."

Both Emily and Timmy finally lost some of their enthusiasm after learning it would be after Christmas and close to school being out before the baby would arrive. That week Amanda and Josh drove the kids to school on a

Friday since that was the only day of the week that the doctor was there.

The kids were in school when Ira came over with a blackberry pie that his wife Alice had made. Amanda exclaimed, "Oh, my, what a pleasant surprise! Please tell Alice how very kind it was of her to make us a pie." Ira replied, "We wanted you both to know how excited we are about your great news!" "What great news?" Josh asked, puzzled. "About the baby," said Ira. "How did you know?" Amanda slowly asked. "Your kids were so excited yesterday at school that that was all they wanted to talk about." "Oh!" Josh and Amanda exclaimed in unison. Neither of them had even thought about their kids saying anything. Now there was no reason for them to make their big announcement. In a town as small as this one, the news would have spread as fast as that forest fire had.

After Josh and Amanda both had a laugh, imagining their children excitedly spreading the news, Amanda excused herself and went into the kitchen. Josh asked Ira if he had time to stay awhile so they could talk about something. Josh explained that with the baby on its way, school going on, winter weather coming, and the upkeep and isolation of the cabin, that he and Amanda had talked about asking him if he would consider selling the house to them. Josh also explained that they would have to add a bedroom and bath which would be a lot easier and less expensive in town. Without hesitating Ira said, "No! You can't buy this house." Josh could not contain the defeated look on his face. But then Ira quickly added, "How can you buy something that's already yours?"

At first Josh was too stunned to speak. Then he asked, "What do you mean?"

Ira said, "Alice and I don't have any family, so with your permission we have adopted your family. Besides," he said with a laugh, "we're too old to worry about the upkeep of this." Josh was overcome with emotion, too close to tears to even say a word. He and Ira talked for a while longer until Amanda came into the room. It was obvious that she had not heard their conversation and when Josh told her, she was so shocked that she could not speak. With tears in her eyes, she gave Ira a big hug, finally able to say, "Thank you, thank you!" Then added, "And Alice too."

After Ira left, Amanda put her arms around Josh and said, "I can't believe it, are you sure this isn't a dream?" Josh laughed and said, "You're the only dream." She laughed, giving him a kiss and then left to see the doctor for another checkup.

When Amanda arrived back home Josh told her that he had a builder coming over in about an hour to talk about the addition. Josh had asked Ira who he would recommend and Ira said that he would use John Boyd, a local man who had some building experience. When John arrived, they explained to him what they would like. After looking at the area Mr. Boyd told them that it would take around six weeks, depending on the weather and availability of material. He gave them an estimate on the price, they shook hands and Mr. Boyd said he would get back with a firm price and could start the coming week. When he had left Josh put his arm around Amanda, saying a prayer thanking the Lord for all that had happened.

The next day they all got ready and went to church where they met Ira and Alice enjoying their usual sweet rolls and coffee as they chatted excitedly about how glad they were to be moving to town. That afternoon they traveled back to the cabin where they would stay until the completion of the home remodeling. Timmy and Emily continued traveling to school in the van each day. Rather than spend the weekend in town the family would only travel in on Sunday. After church Ira would open the store for them to purchase groceries and supplies.

The days were becoming shorter and the weather cooler. There were several rain showers and one had a few snowflakes in it. Josh told Amanda that it was an omen of things to come.

Timmy and Emily went to school each day but Josh and Amanda were reminded that if the weather was hazardous, they would be on their own. Josh and Amanda spent time making sure the cabin was secure and in good shape to survive the winter. Josh collected dead wood left from the fire and made a pile for use in the fireplace while Amanda made sure all the food and liquids that would not survive the cold were ready to take with them when they moved to town. Even though they would drain the pipes, Josh still wrapped them with insulation. The kids were still riding the van but Amanda and Josh were told that in case of snow or ice they would have to take care of themselves.

A few days later while the kids were in school, a storm moved in. By the time they arrived back home the sky was dark and the wind had intensified. Amanda gave them a hug and a snack to eat as they started working on homework. She began to work on preparing supper and Josh turned on the radio. It was announced that there was a certainty that it would snow. On hearing this Josh brought in more logs and made sure the fireplace was ready. He also checked both the outside and inside of the house for any hidden openings. They all sat down for dinner and Emily asked if it was going to snow. Josh told her it might but they wouldn't know until the morning, so they needed to go to bed early. After they finished supper Josh and Amanda got the kids ready for bed and after several kisses told them goodnight.

With the kids in bed Josh went to the fireplace, stoked it and put another log on it. He turned the radio to a station playing soft music then moved the two chairs together in front of the fireplace. Amanda came in with their usual bottle of wine and two glasses. They sat down sipping their wine and watching the dancing flames from the fireplace as they created a soft glow in the room.

Amanda reached over and taking Josh's hand said, "It is so unbelievable and loving to be here with you and the kids." Then she squeezed his hand and looking into his eyes, softly said, "I never thought I would know this much happiness. I love you so."

Josh replied, "I thank God for bringing you into my life and giving me the ability to love again."

They took another sip of wine then arose and holding each other tightly, swayed to the music. Josh whispered, "I know what Heaven is like." He squeezed Amanda and said, "I hope you are enjoying this." Amanda laughed, replying with a kiss, "You are my everything."

They danced for a while longer then decided it was time for bed. As they were lying there holding hands, Josh gave thanks for the wonder, joy, contentment, and love he was given.

Upon awakening, Josh went to the window and peered through the blinds on an enchanting pristine vista of pure white. The sun's rays striking the ice crystals made it look like a field of sparkling diamonds. Not wanting to wake Amanda he went into the kitchen for coffee and a pen and pencil. When Amanda came in, she caressed Josh's shoulder and kissed the back of his neck, then poured a cup of coffee and went to sit down. In her chair was a note.

> I wake up on a cold, snow filled winter morning. Raising the blinds, I peer out on a beautiful vista of pure white. Only yesterday it was multicolored composite filled with imperfections. I feel the cold until I turn and see you asleep and realize that our love, like the snow, covers all

life's imperfections and my heart fills
with warmth.

Amanda gave Josh a kiss on top of his head and whispered, "I love you so much. You warm my heart on a cold winter day."

The kids came in wanting to go outside. Amanda laughed telling them they had to eat first, then dress in warm clothes. Begrudgingly they obeyed. Finally, they could not wait any longer and went running out into the snow with Rowdy in hot pursuit. The snow was only a few inches deep but the kids were not slowed down. They had snowball fights and built a small snowman while Rowdy ran in circles chasing imaginary squirrels.

Josh and Amanda stood with their arms around each other looking out the window at those precious children enjoying themselves. How he wished it could always stay this way. Josh knew that although there would be other grand times, this was one burned indelibly into his heart. "I don't deserve this much happiness. Thank you,

Lord," Josh said. Amanda gave him a hug, then nodded her head in agreement, resting it on his shoulder.

CHAPTER 21

The next two days the kids were at home. Over that time the snow had dissolved into stained, milky colored patches. Timmy and Emily worked on homework, played games on the computer and romped with Rowdy.

When the weekend came Amanda and Josh loaded the truck with some items that were not staying, then they all went into town. Upon arrival, the first thing they did was to check out the addition. They were excited to see that there were only a few minor items left to do. As they entered the baby's room, they were shocked to see a beautiful baby bed. Opening a card lying on the mattress, they read that it came from all of the members of the church.

When they went to Ira's to purchase a few things, mainly cleaning supplies, they excitedly told him how much they appreciated the crib and that they looked forward to thanking everyone at church the next day. Ira gave Timmy and Emily an ice cream cone and told Josh and Amanda to let him know if they needed anything. When they came back to the house the kids went to play with some of their new friends while Rowdy went in the back, much to the dismay of the poor squirrels. Amanda went to the doctor's office to be checked out and was assured everything was okay.

The next day all four went to church where they thanked everyone for the incredible baby crib. Pastor Abbott and the congregation expressed their excitement regarding their moving there on a permanent basis. After the service there was the usual bring-a-dish meal, but this time they were the surprise guests of honor.

On Monday the kids went to school on the van as usual, while Josh and Amanda finished packing up the loose items. One of the church members was coming with his truck to carry everything to the house. Josh and Amanda had decided to leave some of the furniture so they could always come back to the cabin without hesitation. They went through the cabinets and closets. Josh turned off the water and drained the lines and toilet. Amanda propped open the refrigerator door and made sure everything was done.

The man arrived with the truck and everything was loaded. Josh had left June's ashes and the poem he had written for her on the fireplace mantel. As they double-checked everything and prepared to leave, Josh handed Amanda a poem he had written for this occasion.

My love, the two of us on our own over
the years have tried to climb many of
life's mountains. Sometimes the trail
allowed us a modicum of success and
other times dire consequences. Still,
we kept trying to reach the peak.

Now my darling, we are on our last
climb. The view is spectacular but
the snow is falling, often hiding the
trail and making it treacherous. The
difference is that we are now
together, helping and encouraging

one another. The peak is in sight. Soon we will stand on the crest, looking out at the peaceful scene displayed around us. Hand in hand, we will enter the verdant valley, never to climb again.

Amanda reached out and took his hand, then said, "As long as we're together it will be the best." Then added. "We better go, Ira is probably tired of the kids by now."

Josh laughed. "Besides, he is probably out of ice cream."

He went over to turn off the radio before its battery ran out. As he reached to do so the announcer said, "Today's weather forecast calls for clear to partly cloudy."

Josh looked at Amanda and said, "You know that's like life. Most of the time the sun is shining but every once in a while, clouds come along and change everything." He thought for a moment, then said, "It's about how we handle those storms that make all the difference." He turned off the radio, then giving her a kiss said, "Let's go home."

Hand in hand they went out the door to begin a new life.

THE END

Made in the USA
Monee, IL
04 October 2023

43957116R00116